MASTER OF CONTROL

SIENNA SNOW

GODS OF VEGAS BOOK 5

By Sienna Snow

CHAPTER ONE

Present Day
Sebastian

I was a bastard. I knew it. And within the next few minutes, so would she.

I'd spent the last months seducing and fucking the woman I was about to marry.

Most people wouldn't see this as a problem, but then again, they hadn't spent the past five months pretending to be someone else. Someone who wasn't the devil she believed her fiancé to be.

I stared at my reflection in the holding room of Berlin Cathedral, knowing the minute her beautiful cobalt gaze landed on me, there would be only two possible outcomes. One, she would refuse to go through with the wedding, which would start a war neither of our families could afford. Or two, she'd marry me and hate me for the rest of my life.

Either way, I was fucked. And not the kind that left me coming deep in her cunt.

I wasn't the type of man to show weakness or to care what happened to others. The ends always justified the means. Now I was going to lose the only thing that mattered to me outside of taking down the empire my father had inherited on the ashes of my dead mother.

"Sebastian, you ready, son?" a voice said in polished German from behind me.

I shifted my focus to the tall, dark-haired man who looked more like me than my own father.

"I'm ready." I took a deep breath. "Wish me luck."

My uncle Fredrik studied me and shook his head. "You made your bed, boy. Now it's time to face the consequences. If you even want to think about taking the reins from your father, you'd better marry the Benz girl. Whether she hates you or not is insignificant. You hear me?"

Fredrik was the only one in my immediate family who knew what I'd done. I'd confessed the mess I was in after the last time I'd seen my bride. Guilt made a man do some crazy things. Among them was telling my uncle, who was a stickler for behavior, how I'd spent the last few months lying to the woman who owned my soul.

Now here I was, a man who hadn't believed in love, who hadn't believed in anything but the end goal, ready to face the fact he was about to lose the woman who made him want more than vengeance.

"I hear you. One way or another, there will be a wedding today." I just hoped it wouldn't be a forced one.

"Let's go. Your *Vater* is waiting."

Yes, it was always good not to keep the egotistical bastard waiting.

I followed my uncle through the ornately decorated halls of the cathedral and up the aisle to the front altar. *Pater* Joseph waited in his robes for me to approach.

I'd confessed all manner of sins to him since childhood. He understood the world my family encompassed and never batted an eye. He also gave me his unique style of pressure to get me to pursue things outside of the family businesses.

Near him stood my second-in-command and best man, Lucas Flynn. He shook his head as I approached, knowing the shitstorm about to take hold. I ignored everyone else in the packed church, accepting my fate.

Pater Joseph gestured to his left, which was the right of the church, and said, in his singsongy German voice, "The Lord is with you. It's a good day to marry."

If only the man knew the truth.

I took my position and waited. The music from the organs started and the doors opened.

The second my bride came into view, her eyes landed on mine. Knowledge and pain filled her dark-blue gaze.

I was well and truly fucked.

CHAPTER TWO

Eɪɢʜᴛ Mᴏɴᴛʜs Until the Wedding
Sebastian

"You'll marry her if it's the last thing you do."

I stared blankly at my father as he sat behind his giant desk with his hands propped on his bulging belly.

He glared at me as if he were the master of all he surveyed and I'd better fall in line.

The last thing I would do was agree to marry some prim, proper, over-pampered princess who would be more of a liability than an asset. For the past however-many generations, every marriage in the Weber family had been arranged by the patriarch. I'd believed I was home free, since Jonas Weber could give two shits about me or my future.

Besides, I wasn't in the market for marriage, and I

definitely wasn't in the mood to indulge one of Jonas's delusions of grandeur by resurrecting some archaic family tradition.

Yes, he was the head of Weber International, the construction conglomerate that could make or break any development project in Germany, but he hadn't gotten there without my help.

Until I'd taken over the day-to-day operations using my connections and ties, Jonas Weber had been nothing more than a Berlin mob boss with limited reach outside his territory.

But to hear the man speak, he made it seem like he'd singlehandedly created the empire he proudly ran. Left to his own devices, the family would have fallen to one of the rival organizations vying for position in Berlin before I hit twenty.

If my grandfather, *Opa* Steven, hadn't made me promise on his deathbed to keep the family going, I would have turned my back on the whole thing before I'd started college in America. Nothing was holding me to the city, family, or country of my birth. My grandfather was dead, my mother was dead, my sister was dead.

All because of the bastard sitting across from me.

My vow to *Opa* Steven was the only reason I was willing to put up with my father's bullshit demands. How someone so great as my grandfather could have sired a loudmouth know-it-all for a son, who sat on his ass instead of getting his hands dirty, was beyond me. It would shock me if Jonas Weber even knew how to shoot a gun.

"The last thing I need is a bride. I won't have some debutante kidnapped as a way to get back at our family."

"Don't argue with me, boy. This is done. You will do as I say."

"I run the business. I call the shots. What makes you think I'm going to fall in line because you ordered it?"

A calculating gleam entered my father's eyes. "I know you'll do as I say because you want the glory. Everything you've done to date is in my name. And if you ever want full control, you will marry Russo Benz's daughter."

"I will not."

He slammed his fist on the table. "You will, and you will do it with a smile. I don't care if you marry her and only fuck her one time to get the deal sealed, but you will marry her."

"Give me one good reason I should comply. I don't need you."

"You want me to step down. I'll do it within a month of you taking your vows."

This was too easy. There was something else he was up to.

"I don't buy it. You'd never give up the power. You like it too much."

A scowl marred his face. I was the only one around who told him like it was and wasn't afraid of him ordering a hit on me. The men he would order to take me out were loyal to me and would turn a gun on Jonas before even thinking to do anything to me.

"Any man who says he doesn't like power is a liar." He paused. "I have a deal for you."

"I'm listening."

The smirk on his face said he believed he'd gotten my compliance. "You've spent the last ten years trying to find out who murdered your whore of a mother. Well, I'll give you the name."

I clenched my jaw, holding in the urge to punch him.

"And you're the pussy who allowed his wife and daughter to be raped and murdered." I struck his ego with deliberate coldness.

The best way to get under Jonas's skin was to deliver a blow with calm calculation. He'd never had the discipline or the skill to counter these kinds of blows.

Opa Steven had taught me the only way to manage the family was to keep emotions locked away, never reveal any weakness, and most of all, never, ever let temper guide decisions.

Jonas's face grew red. Bringing up my baby sister Hannah always struck a nerve. She was his one love, not his wife, or me. Hannah had been a light in a house full of anger, full of demands, and full of hate. I never begrudged Hannah for escaping the "discipline" Jonas had wielded on me in order to turn me into a man. Hannah had been the one to hide me when Jonas was pissed off about one thing or another. She would find some way to redirect Jonas away from me.

"It was your mother's fault Hannah was with her that day. She's to blame."

"And you did nothing to protect either of them."

The day my mother and Hannah were taken, their usual security detail was on assignment for Jonas. In their place was a group of new recruits into the family. Sending anyone without experience to protect the wife of a mob boss was beyond stupid, and yet Jonas viewed his wife's life as expendable. The fact Hannah had decided to go along on their shopping trip wasn't anyone's fault. From everything I'd learned after I'd returned home, it was Mama and Hannah's biweekly outing that Jonas should have known about.

"There was no way to know she wasn't meeting her lover."

Jonas would constantly accuse her of cheating. Everyone knew it wasn't true. Mama was watched day and night because of Jonas's paranoia.

Mama had been originally promised to my uncle and my father's older brother, Andrew. The two had been friends since they were teens and fell in love as they grew older. The match had been a perfect way to align neighboring families. When Andrew was killed in a territory war with a rival, *Opa* Steven rearranged the marriage contract for Jonas. In the beliefs of the families, one son was as good as another when it meant keeping the peace.

It wasn't until after the marriage that *Opa* Steven and everyone realized what a fucked-up, sadistic bastard Jonas was. The vibrant woman people would describe my mother as being disappeared, and the only important things in her life became Hannah and me. Even if she were having an affair, I wouldn't have faulted her for seeking some semblance of comfort in the world of abuse she lived in.

"There was no lover. It was your paranoia for the fact your wife loved your dead brother more than she ever cared for you. You had the chance to get them back, yet you sat in this office and let them be slaughtered."

"Webers do not negotiate. Arabella knew the danger of going out in the middle of a war."

The peace, or relative peace, the family had enjoyed for twenty-five years under *Opa* Steven had disappeared within months of Jonas taking over.

"That's right—you like to pretend you had no choice by blaming the victim for your lack of balls."

This was getting boring. It was our normal interaction. Jonas ordering me to do something and me ignoring him. For some reason, he hadn't thrown me out of his office by my second retort.

Might as well end it now. I had an assignment to get to, and sparring with this asshole was keeping me from preparing. If only I could tell this dipshit that in addition to running the business he had neglected, I worked as a spy for Interpol, the very organization looking to take him down. My connections and position gave me access into areas it would take others ten times the manpower.

I was just about to stand and tell Jonas to fuck off with his plans and digs, when he pulled out a gun and pointed it in my direction.

His face was determined, but he wouldn't pull the trigger. He needed me too much. I held his glare.

"You will marry that girl. You will expand our holdings. And you will fall in line."

"As I told you. Give me one good reason why I should do anything you say. The way I see it, the only one benefiting from this is you."

"No, boy, it's about you. How badly do you want to find out who killed Arabella and Hannah?"

"Why would it matter to you now? You never tried to look before, and by the time I could, the trail was cold."

"That's not true. I damn well looked. I lost my little girl. I used every connection to find the bastards who did it." His voice cracked, surprising me.

That was the first I'd ever heard about him looking. But then again, I'd been away at university in the States. Finding out Mama and Hannah had been killed after being kidnapped had nearly destroyed me. If *Opa* Steven hadn't kept the knowledge of their deaths from me, I would have been on the next flight back to Germany instead of finishing my exams.

When I'd finally gotten home, there was nothing I could do. Jonas had raged about how Mama deserved everything she got but not his Hannah. He'd shown no inclination to find the killers, only laid blame on everyone, including me.

"Let's just agree to disagree. Your efforts were more than likely half-assed, in the exact way you run the family."

"You watch your mouth, boy. I'm still in charge here."

He waved the gun, his movements erratic, making me think he may shoot me by mistake more than intention.

"Boss." One of Jonas's security shifted toward him. "You need him, sir."

Even his own men knew without me running things, they wouldn't have a future.

"Go ahead and do it, old man. Remember, if I survive, one word from me and your life will take a very dramatic turn for the worse. Who do you think our allies are going to align with? You or me?"

Jonas set the gun on the table, gesturing for one of his men to take it. The man immediately complied and wrapped it in a handkerchief.

"To put your plan into play, you would go against your dear *Opa*'s wishes? Or do deathbed promises mean nothing to you?"

How the fuck would he know about the promise? I'd been the only one in the room when he'd asked me to vow to keep the family intact. Which in *Opa*'s world meant keeping Jonas in charge until the next generation was born. Then and only then would I get the reins, even if I ran everything behind the scenes.

"You bugged his room. The man built you an empire and you showed him no respect, even at the end."

"The man, as you say, wasn't the saint you want to believe. His hands were as dirty as the rest of ours. People only respected him out of fear."

And Jonas was probably the shadiest of us all. One day

soon the world as he knew it would collapse. I was laying the foundation, piece by piece.

"We're going around in circles. My answer to your proposal is no."

I rose from my seat and moved to the door.

Right when my fingers circled the doorknob, Jonas said, "I'm not the one who arranged this marriage, I'm the one to enforce the contract."

I turned, not believing a word coming out of his mouth. This whole conversation had been a waste of my time. I was due in Italy for an assignment, and my jet was ready to leave as soon as I made it to the airstrip.

"And who arranged it?"

"Arabella and your *Opa*. The proof's here." He pulled out an envelope and tossed it across the table.

I walked back to the desk, grabbed the envelope, and opened it. I couldn't believe what I was reading.

Ten years ago, only months before Mama's death, *Opa* Steven with Mama as a witness had signed a betrothal contract between Eloisa Benz and me. It was also an agreement to combine all of the Benz territories running from Berlin to the Baltic Sea and west to the North Sea with the Weber holdings. The marriage would create the largest-held territory in Germany.

I ran a hand through my hair. This couldn't be happening. There had to be a way out of it. It was the fucking twenty-first century.

Then *Opa* Steven's words echoed in my head. *"Promise to keep the family going and not stray from the plans I've set in motion. Some things you won't understand and will want to refuse to complete, but you must go through with them. Promise me, my boy. Let me see your* Oma *knowing our family's future is safe."*

Fuck, fuck, fuck.

I had no choice. I never went back on my word. I was going to have to marry this Eloisa Benz. God help both of us. The last thing any woman should want to do was join my family.

CHAPTER THREE

Isa

"Isa, where have you been?" My grandmother pushed me toward my father's office. "Everyone's been looking for you."

I pinched the bridge of my nose. I hadn't gotten enough sleep, and I wasn't in the mood to deal with whatever I'd done wrong today. I wished I was the debutante my parents wanted me to be, but it just wasn't me. So, the best I could do was pretend. Well, at least in public.

"I swear, *Oma*. I haven't done anything this time."

She gave me a skeptical lift of her right brow. "*Hasi*, you know as well as I do your intentions are innocent, but your delivery has much to be desired."

I should've taken offense to my grandmother calling me a soft and cuddly rabbit at twenty-five, but it had been her term of endearment for me since I was a roly-poly baby who could barely walk on my chubby legs.

"Papa only gets offended because I don't do as he says. Women can do work and accomplish something even if they have the option not to."

"It isn't done, Isa. You aren't like other girls. If you were hurt or taken, it would destroy our family."

My shoulders slumped. I'd heard this nearly every day of my life. It was my burden as the only child of Russo Benz, and the fact I was female. If I'd been born the favored gender, none of the restrictions I lived with would have fallen on me.

"I'm not as weak as everyone believes."

Instead of responding, *Oma* kissed my forehead and shoved me in the direction of the hallway that led to Papa's office.

It was a lost cause to get my *Oma* to understand that there was more to my life than finding the right match, or making the right social connections.

The world around us had modernized, but the organized families with generations of history hadn't evolved. I knew without a doubt, if anyone got wind of what I did on the regular, Papa would lock me in this house and have one of his guards on my ass at all times. Thankfully, the protection Papa had assigned to me since I was five was loyal to me. Plus, I paid them a hefty extra salary on top of what Papa gave them to keep my secrets.

I approached the oversized wooden door to Papa's office and knocked.

"Come in, *Schatz*," Papa called from the other side.

No one would believe the man known for his ruthless control of his territory for over twenty-five years used pet names for his daughter.

I entered, expecting Papa to be alone, but Mama sat in a chair across from him. She wrung her hands together and wouldn't look me in the eyes. From the puffiness of her face, it was obvious she'd been crying, and Papa looked no better.

I narrowed my gaze, worry creeping in. Mama rarely, if ever cried.

"What's going on? Is something wrong?"

"You did this. You tell Isa," Papa said to Mama. The anger in his tone told me whatever was going on had been done behind his back. "The last thing I'd ever want was anyone from that family touching my daughter."

What the hell was going on?

"Mama. What did you do?"

Tears spilled down her face. "Please know I agreed to this when your *Opa* was alive. I never expected Arabella to die. I'd never have accepted the contract otherwise."

Arabella? She couldn't mean Arabella Weber. She'd been Mama's childhood best friend but had lost touch when she'd married Jonas Weber. Mama used to say that if Arabella's first fiancé had lived, she would have been happy, instead of miserable with Jonas Weber. The fact that she was kidnapped, murdered, and her husband had done nothing to save her proved it.

Did Mama just say contract? *What the hell?*

"I'm not following. What contract?"

Mama pulled a tissue from the box on Papa's desk and dabbed her eyes.

"Spit it out, Christina."

"I...I..." She hesitated.

"Oh, for Christ's sake. Your mother and grandfather arranged your marriage to Sebastian Weber. I didn't find out the details until Weber sent the contract to us, saying it was time."

"You have to be kidding me. I'm not getting married. I don't even know the man."

Someone had to really be off their rocker to think I'd accept this without argument.

"That's not all. Marrying him means our families are joined. Since I don't have a son, Weber's son will take over the family upon my death. It means your child with Weber will eventually rule everything."

This couldn't be real. No one did that shit anymore. No, that wasn't true—no one in the world outside of families like mine did that shit anymore. But I never thought Mama of all people would agree to this.

"I don't understand. Why would *Opa* do this? Why would you?" I accused my mother. "I was fifteen when this was drawn up. And he was probably...I don't even know how old this guy is."

Her eyes were filled with sadness, but I couldn't care less. She'd never told me, never told any of us, and she put our whole family on the line. My heart ached. She knew I hadn't been a traditional girl from the time I became a teen. I was the exact opposite of what a well-bred princess was.

Instead of responding to the questions I wanted her to answer, she said, "He was nineteen."

"Did he know about it? Was I living all these years engaged?"

"He didn't know," Papa said. "He's about to learn this same news."

"This can't be binding. It's not legal." I refused to accept this as my fate. But deep inside, I knew there was no getting out of it.

"*Schatz*, I'm sorry. The contract was made by the heads of our families. Our honor depends on it. Your *Opa* wanted this and made it so we…*you* could not refuse."

My temper boiled over. "What does that mean?"

"If you refuse, our business, holdings, everything transfers to the Webers. This part is very legal. If you accept, a trust with one hundred and fifty million Euros will transfer into our names. Yours and mine."

"And if he refuses?"

"He won't." The tone of Papa's voice made me think Sebastian Weber was as bad as his father. "He's set to inherit everything. He will essentially control over half of Germany and parts of Poland and the Netherlands. No man would turn this down. Plus, Jonas Weber will inherit his own trust as a retired family head."

My stomach dropped. I didn't want the money. I didn't need the money. I made enough to support myself.

None of that mattered. For my family, I was going to

have to marry someone I'd never met, knew nothing about, and could only guess had a dark side. Who was I kidding? Most men raised in our world weren't the nice, adoring kind. They were ruthless, took what they wanted, and had no qualms about using force, deadly or not.

Papa had always been the exception in my eyes. Then again, I only focused on the man who raised me. Not the mobster I knew he was, with a territory that he expanded and kept in control using whatever force needed for twenty years. Papa doted on me. He would've loved more children, especially a son. But his love for Mama kept him from divorcing her or having a mistress who could give him children.

"I won't do it," I snapped. "I'm not a child to take orders. I have a life, Papa. I'm not ready to marry anyone."

Papa's gaze narrowed, giving me a glimpse of the boss everyone feared. "You will. I won't let a simple marriage destroy everything I've built over the years. Until my dying day, I plan to hold our family together. We all have to make sacrifices. You'll make this one."

"But Papa—"

"Isa, enough." I jumped at the warning. "I've indulged you for far too long. You will do this for our family. You will marry him. And you will use whatever means necessary to gain leverage on that man. I will make him beholden to me, not the other way around."

I just stared at Papa, not believing the change in him. He'd never spoken to me this way.

Yes, I'd grown up in a life of luxury and had been

pampered, but I'd gone to school. Hell, I'd gone to graduate school. And to Oxford, no less. I'd made a career for myself as an art expert with a specialty in appraisal and authenticity. I could tell a fake from the real thing without batting an eyelash, no matter how good a copy. It wasn't the most glamorous job, but it allowed me to work when I wanted and gave me the freedom to focus on my real business, one my father had no idea about, but I'd done it. I'd succeeded in a field dominated by men.

It pissed me off to no end that my value was in my looks, my pedigree, my family. I'd wanted to be the son Papa never had, and it took me a long time to accept that I'd never had a chance in hell of taking over the family empire. The patriarchal way of things was generations old and wasn't going to change anytime soon. But I never expected *this*.

"Let me get this straight. You want me to sell my body to a man I have never met and use my sexual wiles to captivate him and find out anything that you can use as leverage to keep him in line. In other words, I'm a whore who's been sold by my mother and grandfather to the highest bidder."

I couldn't hide the anger I felt toward Mama, and I ignored the wince she gave at my words.

Papa clenched his jaw. Good, I'd struck a nerve, and he hadn't liked what I'd said. He could try that cold, unfeeling manner with everyone else but I knew my Papa was still under the mask he'd donned in front of my eyes.

"Isa, I didn't have a choice in whether I married your

papa either," my mother said in a low whisper. "But we grew to love each other."

"I don't want to hear it." I stood. I had to get out of here before I lost my ever-loving mind. "You knew how I felt. You knew I wasn't the girl who did what everyone expected. I can't be around you right now. Either of you."

I shot Papa an angry glare, and saw a flash of regret before he schooled it away.

I wanted to run away and hide, but where would I go? Besides, I'd never been one to run away from issues.

I turned and stalked to the door.

The second my fingers closed around the doorknob, Papa said, "Your engagement is set. You'll be Eloisa Weber by next spring."

I froze. That was eight months from now.

Taking a deep breath, I glanced over my shoulder. "Then I guess I better start enjoying the last bit of my life as I know it. And I don't want to meet the man until my wedding day. The last thing I want during the next eight months is a constant reminder of who'll own my freedom."

CHAPTER FOUR

Three Months Later
Sebastian

"Good to see you back in town." A large man in a tailored suit approached me as I entered Verberne Schutzer, one of the newest underground clubs in Berlin. Unless a person knew someone or they were invited would they ever hear of the club or gain admission inside. This wasn't the type of place with lines of people waiting outside, and anyone who learned of the location and tried to gain entrance was met with bouncers who were more than happy to explain they weren't welcome.

I clasped his offered hand. "Good to see you again, Justine."

"I see you've gotten some sun. It must be a nice change from the weather here. Let me guess—you were laid out on some tropical beach with cocktails and honeys around you."

If he only knew. My ribs still hurt from my last assignment and I'd just lost my best friend and partner, Adrian Kipos. The fucker had decided to retire from the job, which meant I was left high and dry. I couldn't fault the man. He'd gotten back together with the only woman he'd ever loved and had known any future with her meant he had to leave the lifestyle. But it also meant I'd lost the only man who I trusted without question to watch my back.

Adrian and I'd started at our agencies right out of college. As an American, Adrian signed on with the CIA, and my road took me the way of Interpol. We had our reasons for the paths we'd taken. Mine being the need to take down the man who'd let my mother die.

"You could say something like that."

"I'm glad I could convince you to come check out the new club. The Boss has gone the extra mile with this one." He gestured toward his right. "Let me take you to a table. I'll see if the Boss is available to meet you."

Oh, I was going to meet "the Boss," all right. I wanted to see how accurate the information I'd gathered was to the public image. She was the ultimate liability, and it was better to view her as a target.

We walked down a dimly lit hallway until we reached a heavy metal door. Justine scanned his thumbprint on a reader and the doors opened, allowing the hip-hop beat of the DJ's music to explode out.

"What do you think?" Justine asked as we entered the club.

I'd only seen one other place with this type of clean lines and sharp contrasts of light and dark colors. It was one of the clubs in Vegas run by the billionaire Lykaios brothers. The one thing that made this place different was the blatant sexual vibe. There were subtle sculptures tucked around the place depicting intimate yet chaste images of couples. It was a tease to the senses, as if one had entered a kink club instead of a dance club.

"It's definitely unique. Not something one would expect. But then again, I believe your boss was aiming for this effect on the patrons."

Justine grinned. "Exactly. The Boss has a way of creating an atmosphere that's the exact opposite of what's considered the norm."

"A rebel in the entertainment world."

We stopped near a set of couches strategically positioned in view of the dance floor but far enough away to give a small semblance of privacy.

"It's the only way to stand out in the crowd. Here you go. Make yourself comfortable. Nikita will be here in a few moments to take your order. I'll go find the Boss and let her know to come over."

I nodded. I wasn't sure if Justine realized he'd said "her" when referring to his boss. The owner was known for keeping a low profile, never letting anyone know she was a woman in a business run by men, especially in Germany. The nightclub world was as ruthless as the one I'd grown up in. But then again, "the Boss" was as experienced in the life as I was.

I ordered my drink and watched the patrons of the club. Most were well-to-do, not the typical underground club goers. These people had money. They dressed casually, but the quality and brands of their clothing said enough.

As I took in the decor, I studied the sculptures more closely. They looked more than the average knock-off of an ancient artist's design. One in particular looked exactly like something I'd seen in an auction catalog not so long ago. Either "the Boss" had money to burn or had commissioned a replica that looked identical to the real thing.

The DJ switched the beat of the music to a hip-hop techno rhythm, a sound popular in Europe. The crowd thickened as they tried to find spots to lose themselves in the sounds booming from the carefully hidden speakers.

"Will you need anything else, sir?" Nikita said as she set my drink in front of me.

I shook my head and she left.

That was when I saw her.

This wasn't the well-dressed and well-behaved princess the pictures had made her look like, or the tomboy in baggy pants that left the shooting range after practicing for hours.

She was breathtaking, seductive, with an aura of innocence that made a man want to protect her.

Fucking gorgeous.

Her gaze landed on me, and my breath caught as if she'd knocked the wind out of me.

I couldn't believe this was the woman my mother and *Opa* had picked for me.

Her black hair was loose in large waves, framing eyes so blue that they looked almost artificial. And those lips—they were full, pouty, and gave a man visions of the perfect uses for them. Her fitted dress was conservative enough not to reveal too much but high-fashion enough to look on-trend.

Taking one last swallow of my whiskey, I rose from the couch and moved in her direction.

She watched me take her in, holding my stare. There was a challenge there as well as interest.

When I was a foot away from her, I offered her my hand without saying anything.

After a moment of hesitation, she slid her palm over mine.

The first touch was electric, and my cock immediately responded. Her breath hitched, and heat entered the deep cobalt irises.

Holy fuck. What was happening?

This attraction was nothing like anything I'd experienced before. The caveman side of me wanted to throw her over my shoulder and take her somewhere I could bury myself deep in her and make her call out my name as she came.

This wasn't what I'd expected when I'd come up with my half-cocked idea of meeting my bride-to-be.

I curled my fingers around her small, almost too-delicate hand and led her toward the dance floor. As we worked our way through the crowd, I noticed how people moved aside the instant they caught sight of her. Everyone seemed to know who she was.

I paused near the center of the dancing bodies, turning to face her. She shifted toward me and slid her free arm around my neck. Releasing her hand, I glided one arm around her waist, drawing her closer to me, and the other up her back.

The music around us blared as we moved together, neither of us speaking, only letting this spark between us guide the dance. The press of her body to mine left no doubt of the need coursing through me.

If I wasn't careful, this woman would lead me around by the dick.

She fucking smelled incredible, a hint of something floral and spiced. I resisted the urge to fist her hair and tilt her neck up so I could get a better sniff.

Was she as affected by me as I was by her?

"Why are you looking at me like that?" she asked, breaking the silence between us.

"I'm trying to figure you out."

"What is there to figure out? I'm a woman in a nightclub enjoying a night out."

She slid against me in the rhythm the DJ mixed, and I almost groaned.

"I find that hard to believe, Boss." I gave her a knowing smile, and she returned it.

"So, you're the VIP Justine wanted me to meet?"

"I'm glad we met like this and not as part of your business."

"Like what?" She was playing with me.

"In the way a man who finds a woman attractive and experiences instantaneous chemistry."

Her breath hitched but she tried to mask it.

"Tell me you don't feel it." I pressed her toward me, bringing her face close to mine.

She licked her lips as her gaze held mine. "I can't."

"Why not?"

"Because nothing can come of it."

"I disagree." Before I could say more, a group of women moved around us, one bumping my shoulder.

Almost immediately, a giant of a man moved in our direction. Eloisa shook her head and he moved back to his perch against a pillar.

She had security watching her every move. I should have expected this. Benz was not going to leave his princess unguarded. However, I had a hard time believing he knew about or would allow his daughter to be in the cutthroat nightclub business.

"This is a nice place. Different. Something I'd expect from the Lykaios brothers in Las Vegas."

Anyone in the entertainment industry knew who the Lykaios brothers were. They'd created an empire that catered to the indulgence of Las Vegas, from casinos and resorts to sporting events, shows, and nightclubs. Each brother had his specific focus, with nightlife being Hagen Lykaios's particular vein of interest.

She gave me a brilliant smile that made her beauty more dazzling. "I'll take that as a compliment. I can only hope to garner the success Hagen Lykaios has created. Like his properties, none of my places are the same. Each has a different vibe, but with a more European flair."

Her enthusiasm for her business told me this wasn't some hobby but an actual endeavor she wanted to make a success.

"How many do you have?"

"I don't know you well enough to divulge that information."

"Then get to know me."

"You don't give up."

"No success ever came by giving up."

The music changed and she stepped out of my hold.

"Thank you for the dance."

"I want to see you again," I said as she turned to walk away.

She paused and faced me again. "I can't."

"Why not?"

She closed her eyes for a second, releasing a sigh of resignation. "Because I'm promised to someone else."

Well, I wasn't expecting her to say that. She went with the truth, not a fabrication.

"Promised? As in engaged?"

"Yes, exactly." She clenched her jaw, telling me she was as thrilled to marry me as I'd been to marry her.

"You don't seem happy about it. I thought women were excited when they're about to get married."

She swallowed, and I waited to hear her response.

"It was arranged. I've never met him. I won't meet him until our wedding day."

"Isn't that a bit archaic? No one does arranged marriages nowadays. And if they did, the couple would at least meet before the big day."

"The world I come from isn't modern. It doesn't follow the rules of society. I'm the one who didn't want to meet. What difference would it make anyway? Any objections to our marriage are irrelevant. Our families will suffer the consequences otherwise."

"You make it sound like your family is the mob and it's about territory." She'd thrown truth my way, I'd do the same.

"I've accepted my fate. I'm sorry we didn't meet sooner. We could have seen where this…" she paused, "…this thing between us could have led. Thank you for the dance."

As she moved to walk away, I grabbed her arm. "What about friendship?"

"Friendship?" A crease of confusion formed between her brows. "I don't follow."

"What if we were friends? Nothing more. I'd like to get to know you."

"I don't have many men who are friends." She looked down to where I held her, the heat of her skin penetrating into mine. "Plus…"

"Plus, what?"

She lifted her gaze to mine. "It wouldn't work. I don't know how to be friends with someone I'm attracted to."

"You're very direct."

"It's the way of things for me. If I'm not, then all anyone would see is the outside and the image my family has created of me."

"So, you know you're beautiful?"

"I look like my mother, so yes. That doesn't mean I want someone to value me for it." There was a slight tone of anger there that told me it was a sore subject.

"Give me your name, at least."

"Isa." She glanced at her watch. "I have to go."

There was a hint of panic in her voice. I wanted to push, but I couldn't. I had no rights over her. Well, as far as she knew.

"I'm Baz."

"That's unusual."

"My mother gave me that nickname."

"What does it stand for?"

"That would require you to meet me for coffee tomorrow."

She shook her head. "I can't."

"Sure, you can. Meet me at Emma's around two o'clock tomorrow afternoon. I'm sure you know where it is, since you can see it on the corner of this street."

"I won't be there."

"I can always hope." I held her gaze as I released my hold on her hand and then turned, walking toward the doors leading to the exit.

CHAPTER FIVE

Isa

I entered my apartment around four in the morning ready for a few hours of sleep. I was exhausted from a busy night putting out one fire after another, something to be expected when opening a new club. And I was more than a bit messed up from meeting Baz.

Of all the times in my life to meet a man who affected me to such an intense level, it had to happen after I'd gotten engaged.

Baz made me feel like he could see deep inside me, down to my soul. Where I kept all my secrets.

And he wanted to meet for coffee. As friends.

Was that even possible with a man one was attracted to?

I walked straight into my bedroom, tugging at the

zipper on the side of my dress. Just as I pulled the designer fabric over my head, my phone rang.

Throwing the dress on a nearby chair, I walked back into the living room where I'd dropped my purse.

The ringing stopped.

Pulling my cell out, I checked the display and groaned.

Oma.

This was going to be a long lecture. I'd better get comfortable.

I quickly ran into my closet, grabbed a pair of shorts and a tank, shrugged them on, and then called *Oma* back while crawling onto my bed.

"Where have you been? You should be in bed, not running around town. You're engaged, for God's sake." The irritation in her voice was palpable.

I could admit I hadn't made it easy for my family. Unless I was required to visit for a dinner or a gathering, I avoided them. And even on those occasions, I kept conversation to a minimum and found an excuse to leave early. I wanted to take every bit of freedom I would have before I became *Frau* Sebastian Weber.

The sad part was, I mainly spent my nights working. Yes, it was in my many nightclubs, but it was still work.

"Good morning, *Oma.* Why are you upset? I *am* in bed. It's a bit early for a social call." I yawned, feeling sleep pushing to the forefront of my mind.

"Don't you lie to me. I'm not as naive as your papa, believing his precious girl is staying home every night even though she's being forced into marriage."

I wouldn't say Papa was naive. Over the last month, I'd realized Papa was trying to make up for the whole mess we were in by letting me do what I wanted. He knew I went out every night. I never hid it, but he thought I was with my friends, not running my business. As long as my security reported that I was fine, he left me alone.

"If I were sleeping with someone you would have good cause to keep tabs on me. I'm not."

"You better not."

Her outrage made me want to laugh. But she was beyond old school and so I listened and kept my amusement to myself.

Oma probably thought I was a virgin too. Lord, if she only knew my deflowering had happened under her nose, while on vacation with her in Switzerland.

I'd been seventeen, about to move to university. I'd met an eighteen-year-old son of a diplomat and we'd had a quick fling. We'd both known it would go nowhere with our parents being who they were. In the end, we'd become friends. Friends who'd stayed in touch over the years and then eventually worked together when I'd opened my first club.

"*Oma*, I'm not going to run away. I'm enjoying my life and the freedom I have. Besides, where would I go?"

She remained quiet for a few seconds.

"Don't get into trouble. Your papa and mama have enough on their shoulders."

I clenched my jaw. I hadn't spoken to my mother,

outside of the required responses, since the night I'd found out about the contract.

I still couldn't understand why she'd kept this from me.

Hell, why had she kept it from Papa?

They were the quintessential mafia romance couple whose story would rival the plots of the most popular novels.

"*Oma*, I'm tired. I want to go to sleep."

Oma sighed. "It's not easy for her. She made a vow to keep the truth from everyone."

"A vow to who?"

"It doesn't matter, Isa. Just know she isn't the villain you want her to be. If there's anyone to blame, it's your *Opa*. God rest his soul, the man made decisions no one could argue with. His reasoning for going to Weber will stay with him in the grave."

It had been three years since *Opa* had passed away. I'd loved my grandfather with all my heart. He was rough and grumpy and ruthless, just like Papa was today.

I knew to understand even an inkling of what he'd been thinking, I would have to talk to Mama.

"Do you miss him?"

"Every day."

"Did you always love him?"

Why hadn't I asked that before?

I guessed I'd never known a time when *Opa* and *Oma* weren't the couple who were in love. *Opa* had been traditional, with clear ideas of the roles of men and women, but he'd treated *Oma* like a treasure.

"No, I actually hated him for the first two years of our fifty-three years together."

"What?"

"He had a mistress, and I wasn't going to accept it, no matter who he was. It took two years for him to get his head out of his ass. Once your *Opa* stopped living the life of a bachelor, I gave him a chance."

"And it took you how long to love him?"

"Another year. Around the time your Aunt Carolena was born, I knew he'd changed."

My Aunt Caro was a force of nature, and I adored her. She'd moved to America after her arranged marriage twenty years earlier and never looked back. She was the wife of an investment manager who catered to families like mine. Even though she could have lived a life of pampered luxury, she ran a chain of high-fashion resale shops that specialized in used designer clothing worn once, if ever.

"Do you think there's hope for me?"

Why had I asked that?

I wasn't sure I could ever grow to love a man who held my family's future in his hands.

What would I do if Sebastian forbade me to have my businesses or work?

I knew plenty of women in our world who had to give up everything they'd treasured before their marriages to focus on the needs and wants of her husband and his family.

"There is always hope, *Hasi*."

"Thank you, *Oma*." I released a loud yawn. "I'll see you tomorrow."

"Now get a few hours' sleep. You'll need it."

What was happening that I'd need sleep? Mama and Papa couldn't spring another surprise marriage on me.

"Why?"

"Your future father-in-law is going to meet the family for brunch at noon."

My lids shot open. "What?"

They must not have understood that when I'd said I didn't want to meet my future husband that it also extended to his family.

"You heard me. Don't be late. Good night." She hung up.

With this new bit of news, I was not going to have any sort of relaxing sleep.

Around twelve thirty, I arrived at El Pesto, an Italian eatery outside the posh neighborhood where my parents lived and I'd grown up. I was late and expected annoyed glares from my family. I was never late to anything, and the fact I was late would mean they thought I'd done it on purpose.

How was I to know that today of all days I'd hit traffic because of a major accident on the road from my apartment to the restaurant?

Honestly, I couldn't say I was too upset. The last thing I

wanted to do was have brunch with the man who'd decided it was time I became his son's wife.

A tall, rail-thin man with salt-and-pepper hair rushed toward me. "Miss Benz. Welcome. Your family is waiting in the Parlor Room."

"Good to see you, Romy. How are the girls?" I leaned forward, kissing his cheeks.

Romy had been my family's personal waiter since the time *Opa* ran the family. He knew everyone's likes and dislikes and had an uncanny way of anticipating the needs of his guests.

"They're very good. Thank you for asking." He led me through the main dining hall and into a back hallway.

Papa and Mama never ate in public unless they wanted people to see them. They preferred privacy and the comfort of knowing people weren't constantly watching them.

I'd heard Jonas Weber viewed attention very differently. He loved media coverage and went to great lengths for everyone to see him. At least his son wasn't of the same mindset. I'd spent the last month scouring the Net for every tidbit of information about him. I'd gone as far as to contact my friend Ana, who recently retired from Solon, a security agency specializing in underground information, to help.

After Ana had gotten over her initial shock of me asking her, she'd agreed to help, but had warned me that her information would be limited since she no longer "officially" worked for Solon.

With who my father was, we tended to avoid discussion revolving around her job or anyone connected to my family.

The information she'd found was limited at best, centered around what was publicly known about him, his family ties, education, and various businesses.

The few pictures of Sebastian available were grainy at best and could have been of any other man on the street. It almost seemed as if he'd scrubbed any and all records about himself.

There was one bit of news revealed in the report that had surprised me. Sebastian had a deep-seated hatred for anyone involved in human trafficking. If he learned any of his associates were rumored to have ties to that world, he made it a mission to destroy that individual and the organization they were associated with.

According to Ana, Sebastian had a reputation for using his connections to work with and help groups whose sole purpose was to end this dark underworld practice.

At least that was something positive about Sebastian Weber.

Papa had the same belief and gave considerable donations to organizations who helped victims who were rescued from sex-trafficking rings.

So in the end, what I'd learned about Sebastian was that he was a ruthless mob boss with a moral compass. Which really gave me no insight into the man himself.

He was a bigger mystery than ever.

I'd asked my family not to meet him or learn anything

about him until we married, and I guessed the universe was answering my request.

Then there was the man I'd met last night. He was another enigma. One I shouldn't be thinking about at all.

Especially when I was about to meet my father-in-law.

Jonas Weber was no way near as big a mystery as his son. Jonas had more than an encyclopedia's worth of information available. I'd learned from listening to conversations over the years that people viewed Jonas as lazy and untrustworthy, and that he possessed an inflated ego. The very type of man Papa despised with a passion.

"Here you go." Romy opened the double doors leading into the private dining room.

Papa, Mama, *Oma*, and Jonas Weber were seated around an oval table. Everyone's attention shifted from the conversation they were engaged in to me.

"I apologize for being late, Papa." I moved toward him.

He rose, meeting me halfway. He engulfed me in his arms for a tight hug and a kiss on my cheek.

"No need to apologize. I heard about the accident on the news reports. Come, meet Jonas Weber."

I approached the man who looked much younger than the sixty-eight years the Internet reported him as being. He had a slight dusting of gray at the temples with the rest of his hair being a rich blondish brown. His build was similar to Papa's, but he wasn't as fit. Something told me he spent more time behind a desk than out with his men.

Jonas took my hand, bringing it to his lips. "So, you are my new daughter."

"Not yet, but soon." I gave him a polite smile. Something about the way he looked at me made my skin crawl.

Oma must have noticed my reaction and spoke up. "Isa, come sit with me. You just missed your fiancé."

My heartbeat spiked. "He was here?"

I moved around to where *Oma* sat and shot Papa a look, but he ignored me.

"Yes, but he had pressing business to attend," Jonas added as he took his seat. "It's something you'll have to become used to. As a Weber, you'll have responsibilities and a role to play."

I was beginning to dislike Jonas Weber more than I already had.

"Isa is a fine hostess." Mama glanced in my direction without actually catching my eyes. "We've raised her well, and she knows what's expected of her."

"I'm sure it's all fine and well, but everyone knows she's been doted upon by the family since you couldn't produce more children. She'll need to have a solid backbone."

"My child has a will of steel. Don't mistake her beauty and delicate size as any indication of her nature."

Were they really talking about me as if I were a head of cattle up for auction?

"She is a pampered princess. We'll teach her what she needs to know to be a true Weber and what will become her responsibilities."

Oh, hell no, he hadn't just said that.

"I'm well educated, beyond you and even what your

son has achieved. I run an art foundation as well as various charities. I know exactly how to deal with responsibilities." My tone wasn't per se hard, but it conveyed I wasn't going to let Jonas Weber bully my family. "You're my future father-in-law, not my future husband. Your input on my behavior and responsibilities isn't requested or required. Your father purchased me for your son, not for yourself."

I stood, knowing I probably shouldn't have said that. I was so tired of people setting the course for my life. I wasn't going to let this man set the precedent for all our future interactions.

It was better that he knew I was a hellion and not the wimp he assumed I was.

Jonas's face grew red. "I am the head of my family and you will honor me as such."

"I read the contract. The second I say my vows, my future husband is the head of the family. I've done my research." I glanced at *Oma*. "I'm sorry but I don't believe brunch is a good idea."

"Benz, are you going to say anything to this girl of yours?"

"I believe she expresses our sentiment. You forced this on our family."

I felt a surge of pride at Papa's words. He'd stood up for me, even if it went against Jonas.

"No, our fathers did." His lips curved. "As did our wives."

"It makes no difference. You and I both know it never

had to pass. A contract like that isn't binding unless one of the parties tries to enforce it. You want what I've built."

Papa's words had no effect on Jonas. His grin grew. "My son will own everything you built. I win, no matter your belief."

"And on that note, I'll head out. Enjoy your brunch. I'm sure there will be hours of stimulating conversation."

I came around the table.

"Where are you going?" Papa asked.

"I have to do some paperwork at the museum for an appraisal I gave them." I turned my attention to Jonas. "Papa Jonas, I would like to refrain from any and all further interaction with you until after the wedding."

I walked toward the doors.

He rose to grab my hand as I passed him. I wasn't sure what came over me. I twisted, breaking Jonas's hold, and then shoved him back, knocking him into the table, causing wine to spill everywhere.

I ignored the shock on my family's faces.

"Don't ever touch me. The only Weber who'll get that right is the one I was bought for."

I stalked out, not bothering to look back.

When I hit the cold fall air, I felt my heartbeat echo into my ears.

Holy fuck, I'd just about decked a man who was not only my future father-in-law, but a crime boss. The fucker shouldn't have touched me.

Why the hell had Papa thought it was a good idea to have brunch with Weber when I didn't want to meet his son until our wedding day? And why the fuck had Sebastian Weber shown up?

Was it some power play to remind me my wants and desires were second to those of the Webers?

It wasn't as if I could forget my mother and my grandfather had sold me to Weber like I was a commodity.

I decided I needed a drink and made my way to Dimitri's, the bar on the corner of the street.

It was named after the owner, who would be tending bar. He'd given me my first "legal" drink when I'd turned eighteen. It wasn't technically illegal for me to drink wine or beer after I turned sixteen, but it wasn't something well-bred daughters did.

Plus, going to the bar would keep the urge to go to Emma's and see if Baz showed up at bay.

That was another complication I had to keep out of my life. What was the point of tempting myself with something I knew I couldn't have?

I pulled the heavy door open, causing the bell on the door to jingle.

Dimitri looked up from wiping the bar, and immediately a smile covered his face.

"Isa, it's been too long."

I hugged Dimitri as he came around the bar.

"It's hard to make it down here unless I'm visiting Mama and Papa. Especially since I don't live in the neighborhood anymore."

"Yes," he said in his musing way. "Stephan told me the other day. He also mentioned you're doing very well in the art business. I hear you're booked out for the next year."

Stephan was head of security for Papa and well aware I wasn't the princess the world believed me to be. He'd personally kept me out of trouble a time or two when I was a teenager. He also treated me like his own daughter and bragged about me like a proud papa.

I glanced at my own security lead, Jax, who happened to be Stephan's son. Jax was the only one Stephan had trusted to protect me.

"It's good to have people who care about you around. They keep you out of trouble."

Jax coughed at that statement, and I glared at him.

Turning my attention back to Dimitri, I asked, "Do you have any of the Firewater Black Label?"

Firewater was a whiskey with a cult following. It tasted like it had been aged for twenty years but in fact was created in a lab and aged less than a year. The owner of the company, Penny Lykaios, was a genius and happened to be Ana's cousin. Ana had introduced us and we'd fostered a friendship over the years. It was actually Penny and her husband Hagen who'd influenced me to take the jump into the nightclub business. With their guidance and the exclusive distribution contract I'd negotiated with Penny for Firewater, I'd gained an edge in the cutthroat nightlife industry.

"You should know. Aren't you the one who got me on the list for distribution?"

Dimitri pulled the bottle from a cabinet where he held

the reserved spirits he kept for his high-end clients, mainly my father and his circle.

"Yes, but no one's supposed to know that secret. If Papa finds out, you won't get any more bottles."

"No one's here who'd tell on you." He looked up at Jax, who nodded.

Dimitri poured two fingers' worth of the reddish-gold liquid into a tumbler and set it in front of me.

Without a second thought, I shot back the expensive whiskey, letting the alcohol burn down my throat and warm my stomach.

"Another."

Dimitri narrowed his gaze at me but complied.

I drank the second glass back. "Again."

"Only one more."

Frowning, I said, "Fine. You'd hand me the bottle if you were dealing with the shit I was."

"Getting drunk won't solve your issues."

I was surrounded by overprotective men, and the way Jax was staring at me, he would take the bottle from me if it were in my hand.

They weren't the one stuck marrying a man they'd never met to save everything their family had worked to build. Or expected to produce the next generation with a man who may or may not be a horrible human being.

God, I hoped he was nothing like Jonas. The man gave me the creeps on more levels than one.

Picking up the glass, I went to drink down the alcohol

when my gaze landed on the man standing outside the bar windows.

Baz.

His dark, almost black eyes studied me. Immediately, I felt my skin tingle. What was it about this man that made my body react so strongly?

It wasn't just his dark good looks or the body that looked like he'd walked off the pages of a fashion magazine, or the hint of tattoos that peeked from the collar of his shirt. He affected me in a way that made me want to let him do anything and everything to me.

He shook his head, glancing at the glass in my hand.

I lifted a brow and downed the drink.

Baz moved to the door of the bar, pulled it open, and walked in, heading straight for me.

When he was less than a foot from me, he pulled the glass from my hand, set it on the bar top, and said, "As a friend, I believe it's safe to say drinking your troubles away isn't the best idea."

CHAPTER SIX

Sebastian

"And how would you know about my troubles?" The irritation on Isa's beautiful face told me she was ready for a fight.

If we were alone and I wasn't getting glares from the man behind the counter or the giant I knew was her security, I'd have given her the challenge she was throwing down.

Everything told me she was dealing with the aftermath of whatever Jonas had said at lunch.

Fucker had set up the brunch as a way to emphasize his influence on the situation he'd put both families in. The bastard hadn't expected me to show up, or that I'd make it very clear to Benz that I took orders from no one, especially not Jonas.

Then, when one of my spies had sent me a text informing me that Isa had walked out of the lunch angry, I knew I had to find her. Jonas was an asshole. Well, I was one too, but in a different way.

I was lying to the woman I was going to marry. Technically, I wasn't lying, I just wasn't revealing who I was, but I highly doubted she'd view it from my angle.

"After last night, I'm pretty sure I know exactly what troubles you."

"Then you understand why whiskey is definitely called for."

"How's that?"

"I just had the pleasure of dealing with my future father-in-law."

I could only imagine how he'd treated her. He thought himself superior to everyone, and his view of women as a whole was low.

I took her hand and pulled her from the bar. "Have coffee with me."

"Aren't you supposed to be at Emma's? That's across town."

I ran a thumb over the pulse point on her wrist, causing her to shiver. She was definitely not immune to me.

"I was about to head there when I saw you throwing back a thousand-dollar-an-ounce whiskey."

That was both a truth and a lie. I'd known she wouldn't have shown up. Her honesty about her life made me realize she wasn't anything like the woman I expected her to be. Her loyalty to her family trumped her personal needs.

When I'd gone looking for her after my call, the last place I expected to find her was drinking her troubles away at a neighborhood bar.

"Well, if I'm going to drink, it might as well be something worth the effort or the possible hangover."

"I doubt you ever let yourself get to that point." The woman had a need to control everything.

I'd gauged that last night, and the unhappiness she felt at not having any say in the course of her life.

"Why are you in my neighborhood, Baz?"

"Your neighborhood?"

"Yes, I grew up here."

"I had business in the area." I guided her to a table away from the bartender and her security who seemed way too interested in Isa's reaction to me.

I knew her bodyguard had seen me dance with her at the club last night, but the bartender was also giving a protective vibe. I couldn't fault him. I'd be the same way.

I was positive she didn't want anyone to know the details on how we met, and already knew she kept her nightclub activities as quiet as possible.

I took a seat across the table from her, not saying anything. Her piercing dark blue eyes were a storm of emotions. He hands were flat on the table, pulling at the urge in me to give her comfort.

Maybe it was the combination of strength and vulnerability that she emanated.

"Stop staring at me like that." The temper in her tone made me want to laugh. She'd let me guide her to the table without a word and now she was trying to take control of her body's reaction to me.

"As I said, drinking your troubles away isn't the best way to let go."

She didn't seem the type to drown her worries in alcohol. But then again, any encounter with Jonas could push a person to measures they'd never think of doing in other circumstances.

"I wasn't drinking my troubles away. I was calming my temper. I'd have to drink half the bottle to get a good buzz. Those three shots did nothing to me."

"Built up a high tolerance?"

"You could say that. The owner of Firewater, Penny, is my close friend's cousin. I had to learn to keep up with the pint-sized genius. Plus, I don't like to be out of control, so I refuse to get to the point where I am."

Figured she would have some ties to the Lykaios family.

All of a sudden, it hit me that Isa had mentioned Penny's cousin. Fuck, it had to be Ana. Ana had just married my ex-partner, Adrian, and we'd shared her not so long ago. It had been during an assignment, but that wouldn't matter to Isa. I'd slept with one of her friends.

I couldn't fault her if she wanted to shoot me when she found out. It would piss me off if she'd slept with someone I knew, let alone a friend.

"You're doing that stare thing again. Stop it."

Ignoring her order, I gave one of my own. "Lay your hands on the table, palms up."

Fuck, what was I doing? I'd met her less than twenty-four hours ago and I was ready to push her in a direction I probably should wait to go.

She narrowed her gaze at me. "Why?"

"Just do it. If what I do makes you uncomfortable then I'll stop."

She licked her lips and then followed my order. Some of her compliance was curiosity but the other part was her response to me.

The second the backs of her hands touched the table, I set mine over hers, holding her wrists under each palm. Immediately, her breath grew unsteady and her eyes dilated.

Her response mixed with touching her in this way had my cock jumping. She had no idea what she was. No. It was more likely she ignored that part of herself, not wanting to entertain the idea she wanted to give up control.

"What are you doing?" Her words were unsteady.

I gave a slight squeeze of pressure causing her to shift in her seat.

"I'm in charge now. You can't leave unless I let you go. Everything pressing has to wait."

I knew as well as she did that with one word, her security would be over here and putting me in a headlock.

"We shouldn't be touching like this."

"Then tell me to let you go." I held her gaze. "All you have to do is say stop."

The indecision warring in her eyes made me realize how much she needed this.

"Look at me, Isa."

Her blue gaze shifted from where I held her wrists to my face.

A crease formed between her brows. "I don't understand why I listened to you. It makes no sense."

"Have you ever let any of the men you've taken to bed be in charge?"

A twinge of irritation entered my mind at the thought of anyone having ever touched her.

Yes, it was irrational, but knowing this was the woman who was going to be my wife and the intense pull we had to each other brought out the caveman in me.

"What does that have to do with anything?"

Her response was all I needed to confirm my suspicions and ease my annoyance.

"Did you leave feeling unsatisfied, feeling like you were missing something?"

She opened her mouth to deny my claim but shut it.

She knew the truth as well as I did.

"Tell me, Isa, if a man took all the control, bent you to his will, and gave your mind and body unimaginable pleasure, would you let him?"

Her breathing grew ragged and she swallowed to ease the arousal I saw flushing over her skin.

"I can't do this. I'm going to marry someone else," she said, shaking her head. "It's...it's... I have to go."

My fingers tightened before she could pull free.

Isa closed her eyes. "Baz, don't make me want things I can't have. It's cruel."

"Why is it cruel? You should admit, at least to yourself, the true nature of your desire."

"And do what with it?" The anger in her voice surprised me. "I'm about to marry a man I don't know or love. Who knows what he'll be like?"

I studied her, not releasing my hold on her.

Fuck. I was going to fuck this up. Hell, I'd already screwed up beyond repair. I was lying to my fiancée. I was…God, I had no idea what I was doing. All I knew was that when everything came out, she'd hate me.

I wasn't supposed to have this need for her.

"What if you react to him the way you do to me?"

"It doesn't matter how I react to you. Nothing can come of it. I'm marrying another man." This time she managed to pull free of my hold. "I can't throw away my family's future for whatever this attraction is."

I remained quiet, not knowing how to get out of the hole I'd dug for myself.

"I offered friendship. I still stand by it."

"It won't work."

"Try it, Isa. Friendship."

Maybe if she saw the real me then she'd accept me when she learned the truth.

Who was I kidding? I was fucked beyond repair.

"Friends. No expectation for anything else. No touching me. And no more conversations like the one we just had, or I won't see you again."

"Done."

At that moment, Isa's security approached.

"We have to get you home so you're rested," the man said.

"I guess it's hard to balance a daytime life and a secret nighttime one."

Her lips curved slightly. "You could say that."

"When do you get up after a long night?"

"It depends on the day and if I have an antiquities project. Tonight, I won't go to bed until at least seven in the morning so I'll sleep until noon."

"Then meet me at Emma's for coffee."

"You're serious about this friendship thing, aren't you?"

"Why are you surprised? I mean what I say."

She sighed. "Fine. We'll give this friendship thing a try."

I sa

I yawned as I walked the street leading to Emma's. I wasn't sure why I was doing this. Maybe it had to do with wanting to rebel against my family, the Webers, the world.

I knew nothing would come of anything with Baz. Hell, I didn't even know his last name. Well, I guessed he didn't know mine either.

How would he react when he learned it? Would he

know I was the daughter of the man who ran most of the streets of Berlin? Would it matter?

I wasn't planning on hiding it. There was no point. Papa was too much of a public fixture. Luckily, Papa did everything to keep me out of the spotlight. And if anyone managed to link us, I'd act as if it were no big deal. I guessed it also helped that I'd spent years living in the United Kingdom and Switzerland.

My phone beeped with an incoming text. It was from my best friend, Lilly.

Lilly Lennox was the daughter of one of my father's associates, though we hadn't known it at the time we'd met in graduate school. We ended up working on a research project together and became fast friends. Now three years later, we ran an antiquities company together.

Lilly was not only my partner but the only person who understood the world I lived in. She knew all my secrets, from the clubs to my relationships with groups our fathers would lose their shit over if they ever found out. I never gave her details on said groups, but she was a smart girl and probably had some inkling. Besides, it was better to keep her out of the nitty-gritty details. All she needed to know was that anonymous clients hired us to appraise art pieces and verify authenticity.

We both got to play sleuths without actually leaving our office. Plus, Lilly was a free spirit and viewed the world through rose-tinted glasses. She wanted to believe the best in people. She kept me from getting lost in my businesses.

The last thing I'd ever do was put her in any form of danger.

Her father knew his daughter didn't fit the typical princess role. Lilly with her whimsical clothes and wild hair would fit more into a hippy colony than the streets of Berlin.

Lilly: *I finished the appraisal. The fee is in our account. Ana sent notice that she isn't going to be our auction house contact anymore.*

I wasn't happy about the change. Hopefully, whoever replaced her was easy to work with.

Ana was the one who'd pushed me into working for her "company," in a consultant capacity. The company, also known as Solon, was more than an average business. It was one that required security clearance and an intense background check. The fact I had ties to the "unsavory" elements of society had been a positive instead of a negative to Ana's boss, Bri, who had hired me for my first project.

Being a mobster's daughter had its benefits, especially when working as an informant/appraiser for various secret agencies from Interpol and the CIA to underground ones like Solon. They had no qualms associating with me, and it was understood, for my assistance, they would keep any and all operations managing my father's business dealings far away from me.

I crossed the street and typed out my response.

Ana leaving was something I'd expected after talking to

her and reading a report giving a general case analysis of Ana's last assignment.

She'd been part of a multi-agency case that had taken a turn no one expected. The sex traffickers they were targeting had kidnapped her and put her up for sale. If it wasn't for her now-husband, Adrian, a CIA agent, and his Interpol partner, she would have been sold to God only knew who.

She'd had to play the role of sex slave for Adrian and his partner. Whatever she'd experienced had changed her plans for her career in Solon. Now she was back in Las Vegas, helping run her family's businesses.

Isa: *She just got married and has a baby on the way. I think she has other priorities on her mind than working with us.*

Lilly: *Does this mean you're going to follow in her footsteps? After all, you're getting married in a few months.*

Isa: *Hell, no. My work isn't going to suffer because of decisions made by my family.*

Lilly: *Good luck with that. I'm sure your new husband is going to be fine with you running nightclubs, appraising artwork for clients with no names, and consulting for "the company" while being his arm candy.*

I scowled at the phone.

Isa: *I'm no one's eye candy.*

Lilly: *Hate to tell you this, but that's exactly what you'll become.*

Isa: *I'll figure something out. I refuse to let anyone control my life.*

Lilly: *Want to meet me for coffee?*

Isa: *I can't. I have plans.*

Lilly: *With who?*

I could totally lie to her but Lilly was my ride or die and would keep a secret.

Isa: *A VIP I met at Verberne Schutzer.*

Lilly: *No fucking way. Who is he? Give me his name, I'll have everything you need to know about him within the hour.*

Lilly was not only an art expert but a secret hacker who could find anything about anyone.

Isa: *It's better you know as little as possible.*

Lilly: *I don't like it.*

Isa: *It's just friendship.*

Lilly: *Right, friendship with a hot guy that you met at one of your clubs. Isa, you're playing with fire.*

Isa: *Stop worrying. It's completely innocent. Besides, I never said he was hot.*

Lilly: *I hope you know what you're doing. I've never known a man and woman to only be friends.*

Isa: *Got to go. I'm at the shop.*

Lilly: *This conversation isn't over.*

I had no doubt she was going to hound me for information until I relented.

I tucked my phone back into my handbag and pulled open the door.

My eyes immediately landed on Baz. He sat in the corner reading a paper.

Fuck, he was beyond gorgeous.

I wasn't sure it was possible for a man to have this level of appeal. He wore a fitted green sweater and a pair of dark denim jeans. The tattoos around his wrist peeked out from the long sleeves, giving him a sophisticated yet dangerous edge.

His manner was eerily similar to the way Papa and his men carried themselves. He even sat in a position that kept anyone from coming up behind him.

As if sensing my study of him, he lifted his dark eyes to mine. My knees went weak, and I felt a flutter deep in my stomach.

No, Isa. This is friendship. Put any other thoughts away.

"Isa. You look beautiful." Baz stood as I approached and gestured to the chair across from him.

He glanced behind me. "No security?"

"Oh, they're here. The only reason you'd know they were around is if they wanted you to know." I took my seat and waited for Baz to take his.

"Good to know."

A waitress came up to us, and I ordered a coffee and a pastry.

"What's your last name?"

Baz lifted a brow. "Does it matter?"

"Friends usually know these things."

"Klein."

I offered him my hand. "I'm Eloisa Benz."

A slight smile touched his lips as he slid his palm against mine, engulfing my hand in his large one. "Baz Klein."

The next hour was easier than I expected. We ate, laughed, and got to know each other. Our conversation never stopped and flowed from one random topic to the next. There was no touching on the subject of my upcoming marriage or the fact we shared a crazy attraction. It was almost like the conversations I had with Lilly.

I learned he was in shipping and a real-estate investor specializing in international projects, that he traveled a lot, and he'd had a tumultuous relationship with his father following his mother's death.

I told him about growing up an only child to overprotective parents and grandparents. And the story of how I ended up in the nightclub business because of a suggestion from Penny and Hagen.

By the time our date ended, we had another coffee date set for the coming week, and I had a comfortable feeling that a friendship between Baz and me was something very doable.

CHAPTER SEVEN

ONE WEEK Until the Wedding

Isa

"So, are you going to tell me more about this guy you're seeing other than his name?" Lilly glanced at the calendar. "Isn't today your regular coffee date?"

I looked up from a painting I was examining and glared at her.

"I've already told you. He's just a friend. We have great conversations. There isn't more to tell."

"I need more details. None of my searches has come up with anyone named Baz Klein."

"You investigated him." I couldn't disguise my annoyance with Lilly. "I didn't give you permission to do that."

What I had with Baz was like nothing I'd ever had with

any man before. We were real friends. He listened, gave advice, and took mine in return. We never crossed any lines. Although the underlying attraction seemed to be growing more intense.

"You've been so vague. I had to find out more about him. Especially with who you are and who you're about to marry. The last thing you need is someone taking advantage of you."

"I'm not stupid. I never go anywhere without protection."

"That's not what I mean, and you know it. I'm worried about your heart."

"For my heart to be involved, it would mean we were meeting to do more than food and conversation."

Now if only it didn't feel as if I was lying. I'd grown attached to Baz, and admitting it to anyone would hurt more than when I told him we couldn't meet anymore.

Something I'd have to do sooner rather than later.

I was on a deadline, and it was a matter of days until my life changed forever.

"You know I'm not going to judge you if you decide to move it to a different level and have a fling before you're shackled to Weber."

"I adore you for saying that, but I'm not going to start an affair with a man I can only be with for a week. I just want us to keep it in the friend zone."

"And I have a bridge to sell you."

"You're such an ass."

Lilly blew me a kiss and went back to studying the sculpture she'd spent the morning examining.

"Yes, but I'm not keeping things from my best friend."

Setting down the magnifying glass I was using to inspect the painting, I said, "Fine. Ask me what you want to know."

"How about what does he do?"

"He works in shipping."

"That could mean anything."

I rolled my eyes. "Does it really matter? It's not like I'm marrying him. I probably know more about Baz than the man I'm actually marrying."

She shrugged her shoulders as if agreeing with my statement and then continued her questions. "How old is he?"

"Twenty-nine."

"On a scale of decent to scorching, where does he fall?"

I paused, thinking about his dark eyes and the sexy tattoos that covered his arms that I'd gotten glimpses of during our last coffee meetup. We'd been debating the perceived value versus the actual value of an art piece that had made worldwide news for the exorbitant price a collector paid.

Baz had insisted the buyer had gotten a bargain and I'd insisted he'd paid too much, when Baz had rolled up his sleeves and set his elbows on the table to make his point. I'd lost all train of thought outside of how sexy Baz was. How he was way too built to be a man who worked in a corporate-type job. It had taken me a full minute to bring my head back into the conversation.

"I take your silence and the pinkish tint of your cheeks as on-fire scorching."

"Whatever."

"Does he know about your marriage?"

"Yes."

"Really?"

"Why would I lie about that? It's not like I can pretend it's not happening."

"Point taken."

"Does he know who you're marrying?"

"No. We haven't touched on the subject since that day at Dimitri's."

We may not have spoken about it, but it lay like a heavy weight between us.

Lilly tapped her lip, lost in thought.

"What else?" I asked, knowing if she got all her questions out that she'd leave me alone and let me finish my work so I could get home with enough time to take a nap.

I had to make plans for the management of the clubs, and I knew it would take me all night to get everything organized with the staff.

"Is he tall?"

"Yes."

"Is he built?"

"Yes."

"Is he smart?"

"Yes."

"Do you want to sleep with him?"

Before I could censor myself, I said, "Yes." I covered my face with my hands. "Forget I said that. It doesn't matter anyway."

"Yes, it does." The adamancy in her voice surprised me. "You're in an arranged marriage to save your family. You're allowed to have some fun."

"I'm not a cheater."

"It's not cheating, and you know it. You haven't even met the man. Hell, you'll meet him at the same time I will. Live a little, Isa. You push the line in all aspects of life but the personal."

"And if I get caught?"

Lilly glared at me. "You know as well as I do that the only way anyone will catch you doing anything is if you let them. You're a sneaky-ass bitch."

"I'm sure that was meant as a compliment."

"I'm serious. Go on a real date with the man, have an affair, make memories you can take into the farce of a marriage your family is forcing on you."

"I'm not sure it's a good idea."

"Of course, it is."

"I can't."

"Of course, you can."

"No, Lilly. I won't hurt him like that or hurt myself. It's going to be hard enough as it is."

"So, it is more than just friendship?" Lilly gave me a smug smile.

I sighed. "It doesn't matter."

"Yes, it does."

She really was like a dog with a bone. Before I thought twice about it, I grabbed my phone and sent Baz a text.

Isa: *I can't see you today. Actually, it's better we don't see each other again. I'm getting married in a week and it's only prolonging the inevitable.*

Immediately a response came, but I set the phone on the counter, not wanting to look at it.

Lilly grabbed my phone and read the message. "Why would you do this? He wants to see you. You have a week more with him."

"I'm not with him, dammit." I snatched my phone back from her, when it began to ring.

The call was from Baz. I ignored it, set the ringer to silent, and shoved my cell in the back pocket of my jeans. "Let it go. I can't discuss this anymore. It's like we're going around in circles. Why don't you worry about your love life and that guy you're seeing?"

Lilly frowned at that. For the last few weeks, Lilly had been seeing this guy she'd met at a party. They had this relationship that blew hot and heavy half the time and cold and distant the rest.

"Don't try to deflect on me."

"Lilly, please." I hadn't expected my voice to quiver.

All of a sudden the weight of everything that was happening in my life hit me. I had no idea what the future would hold for my friendships, my family, my businesses. Everything in my carefully controlled life was in turmoil.

I closed my eyes and pinched the bridge of my nose.

Lilly's arms came around me. "I'm so sorry, Isa. I didn't realize he meant so much to you. I won't bring it up again. I promise."

Dropping my head to her shoulder, I let a tear fall.

"Can we do something tonight? I don't think I have it in me to plan for the clubs. I just need something that will take my mind off everything in my life."

"Are you sure you want to venture into my type of fun?"

"Your version of wild is going bar hopping and getting in bed by one in the morning. I think I can handle it."

Lilly shook her head. "I feel like you don't know me at all."

"Okay, I challenge you to a night on the town where you don't head home the second the clock strikes midnight."

"Challenge accepted."

"Are you enjoying yourself?" Lilly asked as we waited for the crowd to quiet.

"When you said you were going to show me a good time, I never expected you to take me to a kink club."

"Disappointed?"

"No, not in the least."

In fact, I was fascinated. This was a world I'd never dared to explore. A world I knew existed but never wanted to risk seeing for fear of knowing I couldn't be part of it. It was probably why I'd gotten so upset with Baz that day at the bar.

"I'm so glad. Stay here—my favorite couple are about to go on. I'll be back in a bit."

"Where are you going?"

"To find Kane. This is one of the businesses he manages. He wants to meet you."

"I'll be here when you get back."

At that moment a couple stepped down into a sunken stage with a St. Andrew's cross set in the corner. The crowd went silent and all attention went to the people onstage. The Dom and his submissive were beyond gorgeous. The petite female wore a light pink robe and had her long golden-blond hair tied in a ponytail atop her head. The man was tall, over six feet, and built like a wrestler. His clothes were simple: jeans and a button-down shirt, rolled at the sleeves.

When they were in the center, they stared into each other's eyes, as if the world started and ended with their partner. There was love there and trust, complete trust.

He untied the belt of his submissive's robe and then helped her out of it. She wore a black leather bra with straps that crisscrossed her ample chest and a thong made of the same material.

After throwing the robe on a nearby bench, the Dom kissed his submissive and then walked her backward until her back hit the soft cushion attached to the St. Andrew's cross. He stroked her with light caresses as he fastened the cuffs to her ankles and wrists.

Her breath grew ragged and arousal flushed her skin. The adoration she had for her Dom made something ache in my heart.

I'd never experience this, this kind of affection, this type of pure need.

I'd marry Sebastian Weber and enter the role of the respectable wife, whatever that meant. I could only hope he was kinder and less self-centered than his father and we learned to accept each other.

Maybe I should have dug deeper to learn as much as I could about Sebastian. Instead, I'd essentially stuck my head in the sand and pretended nothing in my life was going to change.

I was an idiot, who needed to get my act together.

I had only a few days left to figure out how to keep my secrets from the Webers. I wouldn't put it past Jonas Weber to somehow use it against my family, if he got even a small inkling about my clubs.

Would Sebastian be like Jonas? Cold and egotistical?

Would he treat me as if I were a commodity, to parade around to increase his standing?

How would Sebastian react when he found out what I did outside of art appraisal?

God, my mind swam with so many unknowns.

I hated to even entertain the idea of having to sell the clubs to fit into a role that I'd never wanted in the first place. But I had to be prepared.

Lilly would help me keep things quiet, but she knew nothing about the nightclub business to help me operate them. There were only two people I could call on and no one could ever find out our connection: Ana and Penny. They, with their families, understood the business and would manage everything for me. Hell, Penny's husband Hagen had offered to buy all my clubs a while back when he wanted to enter the nightclub market in Germany, but I'd refused. He'd made me promise that if I ever decided to sell, I'd contact him first.

The slap of a flogger on the Dom's hand snapped me out of my thoughts and brought my attention back to the couple.

The Dom circled his lover twice, whispering things I couldn't make out and then when I least expected it, he smacked the wide leather tails against her breast.

She arched into the strike, begging without words for more.

Over the next ten minutes, the Dom worked every inch of exposed skin on his submissive, bringing forth a light pink flush of color to the surface of her body.

Arousal pooled between my legs, and my nipples beaded.

What would it be like to be the one on the cross, the one to feel the bite of the flogger, the one to be lost in sensation?

I pushed the thought back. There was no point in going there.

I swallowed the lump in my throat.

I shouldn't have come. I should have taken the night off to plan the next months at my clubs.

I had to get out of here.

I scanned the crowd to find Lilly. I couldn't just leave without her knowing. She'd understand. She always did.

"Oh dear God. This can't be happening." My breath caught as my gaze landed on Baz.

He watched me with an intensity that had me shifting where I stood.

What was he doing here? And why did he have to look so good? Or look at me the way he did?

He wore dark jeans with a fitted T-shirt molding to his honed arms. His tattoos weren't covered as they usually were, giving him a dark and dangerous aura and making butterflies scramble in my stomach.

Even that night at my club, he hadn't seemed like such a predator.

And I knew I was definitely prey.

My heartbeat pounded in my chest and the arousal from watching the scene intensified.

Baz mouthed, "Don't move."

Goosebumps prickled my skin as did anxiety. He worked his way around the crowd watching the couple until he came behind me.

His body heat was a brand on my back.

He didn't touch me but leaned down and whispered in my ear, "You stood me up."

"I sent you a text."

"A text isn't good enough. Especially if you're going to tell me we can't see each other again."

I licked my lips. "It's better that way. I'm getting married in a week."

"I thought we were friends." His breath on my neck was more erotic than the scene unfolding in front of us.

"We can't be friends anymore."

His hand settled on my waist, and a tingle shot down my spine. "Why not?"

"You know why."

"You want more."

I kept quiet and clenched my fists, resisting the urge to set my hand over his. If I touched him, I'd want everything I couldn't have.

"I want more too." His fingers flexed on my waist. "I want it all."

"It's not possible."

"What if I say I'm keeping you even if you hate me."

"Please, Baz. Let me go. I should never have agreed to see you again."

"Just as I should never have walked into your club that night."

It would have been better if he hadn't. I wouldn't have ever met him and wouldn't know what I was missing when I married.

Before I could say anything in response, he added, "But fate brought us together."

"Fate fucked up. You came too late."

"Maybe, but then again she did guide you into my club tonight."

I stilled, glancing over my shoulder. "This is your club?"

"Yes." His black eyes bored into mine.

That meant Kane worked for him, and it also meant he had ties to my world.

This was bad. If anyone found out about us, it could mean his life.

"Why didn't you ever mention you owned a kink club?" I shifted my attention to the couple, not wanting to let Baz see my vulnerability.

He cupped my jaw, shifting my face until I was looking at him again, and ran his thumb over my lips. "Because you told me to never have another conversation like the one we had at Dimitri's or you would end our relationship. I wasn't going to risk that and lose my chance to be with you."

"Baz, I can't."

"Can't what?"

"Can't be with you."

"You've said that." He dropped his hand and turned me to face the couple. "Watch them. This is what I meant when I spoke of relinquishing all control. Kiera trusts Liam enough to put her pleasure and pain in his hands. Isn't that what you want, Isa?"

Baz slid his palm across my abdomen, drawing me against his front. I closed my eyes, loving the possession of his touch too much.

I needed to tell him to let go, to not make me want things I wasn't allowed to have.

I searched the floor for any sign of Lilly, with no luck.

"Watch. I want your attention on them. Your friend is with Kane. He'll take care of her."

"Did you know Lilly was my friend?"

"No. Kane said his girlfriend was bringing a friend tonight. Luck had it that the friend was you."

I wasn't sure I'd call it luck but kept that view to myself.

"Watch them, Isa."

For the next few minutes I focused on the couple, the way they responded to each other, to the passion between them. It was sexual and not. It was as if the Dom…Liam could read Kiera by the slightest change in her breath. There was a bond between them, similar to what I'd noticed between other couples in the club.

Need for what they had coursed through me, and having Baz behind me wasn't helping. The press of his hard body, his arousing scent, his dominant hold on me.

Fuck, I was in so much trouble. I was going to do something I knew was destined to lead to disaster.

As the scene ended, applause broke out and the crowd began to shift. But I couldn't move. I was transfixed on the pair. Kiera's eyes were now closed, as if she was lost in euphoria. Liam gently unbuckled each strap, letting her sag against him. Then when she was free, he cradled her in his arms, kissing her forehead and whispering something that had her smiling. After wrapping the robe around her, he carried her out of the area.

Baz remained behind me, his hold just as firm as it was when he'd placed his hand on my stomach.

"You're coming home with me, Isa. Let me give you

what your body needs. What your mind needs. Then we'll talk. Talk through everything."

Talk? There was nothing to talk about when my future was set. All I could do was focus on now, on him, on us for one night. I was going to take something I wanted. I'd face reality tomorrow.

I'd have no choice.

"Take me home, Baz. Give me this one night."

CHAPTER EIGHT

Isa

Baz shifted until he was facing me. "We'll talk. I have things to say. Then you'll make a decision about our future."

"No." I placed a finger on his lips. "Give me everything you promised. If there's time, then we'll talk. But you have to know, I can never be yours. I'm promised to another."

He looked as if he wanted to argue but instead sighed and took my arm, guiding me out of the club and toward his waiting car. Neither of us said a word during the short drive to a tall building overlooking the river.

The second the car stopped, the doorman approached and opened my door.

He offered me a hand to step out and looked at Baz, smiling. "Welcome, Mr.—"

"The keys are in the ignition, Bran," Baz said before the doorman could finish his greeting.

Bran nodded and went toward the driver's side as Baz came around the back of the car.

We stared at each other, the need and emotions of the night heavy between us.

"Ready?"

"Yes."

We entered the lavish lobby of the building and walked straight to a waiting elevator. Baz punched in a code on a keypad hidden behind a metal panel, and immediately we began to ascend.

The cab opened into a large foyer filled with sculptures, pieces that I knew were authentic.

"Want a drink?"

We moved into a very masculine living room with a breathtaking view of the Berlin night sky.

"No."

I wanted to reach for him, but I wasn't sure how this was going to work. I'd never done anything like this. I'd never wanted anyone this desperately.

"Baz. Do something." My words were breathy, revealing the uncertainty and need I was feeling.

He remained across the room, watching me. His eyes blacker than I'd ever seen them before.

A throbbing between my legs pulsed, and my body ached for his touch.

Just when my patience with waiting was over, Baz

stalked toward me, fisting my hair and bringing his lips down onto mine.

Dear God, he tasted incredible, like whiskey and chocolate mixed together.

My arms came around his shoulders and I met his insatiable demands with mine. He ate at my mouth, tasting, biting, consuming me.

I was lost in him, the feel of him, the desire I'd pretended I could push away. If I was going to sacrifice my happiness for my family, I was taking this one moment for myself.

He gripped my ass, pulling my clit flush against his cock.

"Bazzz." I threw my head back, breaking our kiss.

He ran his tongue down my neck and then murmured, "You made your choice. You're mine. I'm going to bury myself deep in your pussy by the end of the night."

"Yes. I want this. I want you. Something that's mine before my world becomes a gilded cage."

He pulled back, a shadow of something flashing in his almost black eyes before he schooled it away and kissed me again.

Baz backed me against a wall, continuing to feast on me.

"I want you out of these clothes. Turn around."

I shifted, facing the wall and pulling my hair over my shoulders. He unzipped my dress and followed the trail of the zipper with his mouth. My skin heated and felt as if it was on fire. I'd never been aroused like this.

The designer fabric slid from my shoulders, pooling at my feet. Next went my bra and underwear.

"You're fucking gorgeous." The deepening timbre of his voice had my pussy contracting.

I glanced over my shoulder and found him watching me. His palms gripped my ankles, tugging them apart, and then he glided his hands up my calves to my thighs. His thumbs teased the valley where my core dipped.

Then he cupped my ass. "Perfect."

Before I knew what he was doing, he pulled his palm back and brought it down on my bottom.

"Baz," I cried out as fire shot through my body, and just as fast, a delicious sting replaced the pain. My fingers pressed against the wall helping me keep my balance. I dropped my head onto the back of my hand, breathing in hard pants.

"More?"

"Yes," I gasped. "I want more."

I wanted so much more.

"Good." His hand landed again and again, peppering different parts of my ass until he'd covered every inch.

I was mad with need, lost in the pleasure-pain.

My core clenched but it wasn't enough. I needed something to send me over.

His warm hand moved up the inside of my thigh until he grazed the lips of my soaked sex. He dipped inside, rubbing up and down, teasing my clit.

"Baz, please."

"Fuck, you're dripping." He hummed. "I have to taste you."

He turned me so fast I almost felt dizzy. Hoisting one leg over his shoulder, he took a long swipe with his tongue. I grasped his head, throwing mine back.

"I'm going to make you scream, *Prinzessin*."

"I'm, I'm okay with that. Sooner would be better than later."

He chuckled as he began his assault on my core. He licked, sucked, and thrust, driving me higher and higher. I writhed against him, lost in the sensation. My legs grew weak, causing me to wobble. Baz grasped my hips and held me against him as he continued to push me toward release. I'd never experienced this level of desire before. My breasts ached and my pussy quivered. I held on to Baz's head, arching into his delicious torment.

He pushed a finger inside me, curling it upward. Immediately, my orgasm burst free as my pussy contracted and flooded with my arousal.

"Baz. Oh God, Baz."

"That's it, baby." He pumped in and out, prolonging the pleasure coursing throughout my body. "Mine. Every one of your orgasms belongs to me."

In the back of my mind, I wanted to tell him this was the only time, but I couldn't say anything. I wanted what he said. To be his, to belong to him, but my fate was set and I had to protect my family.

I slowly came down as Baz wiped his mouth on the inside of my thighs and pulled free of my pussy.

"You taste incredible. I'm going to have to gorge on you again before the night is over."

I gasped, resting my head against the wall. "I really hope so."

"Before we go there, I want to feel you shatter around my cock." He slid my leg from his shoulder and slowly rose to his feet, making sure to keep a firm hold on my hips to keep me from falling.

His face was flushed as I knew mine was, and his breath was unsteady. His lashes looked longer than usual, giving his raw masculinity a beauty that would be out of place on any other man.

"Mine," he said again, drawing me to him and then lifting me into his arms.

He shifted and carried me in the direction of what I assumed was his bedroom. I'd barely had time to notice the dark tones of the room before he laid me on top of the thick comforter.

Pulling his shirt over his head, he tossed it behind him before crawling over me.

His hard-sculpted body was better than anything I could have imagined over the last five months. I wanted to trace the tattoos with my fingers, my mouth, my tongue.

Had I ever seen a body this perfect?

No. None of my past lovers could hold a candle to this man.

"Touch me, Isa. I've wanted nothing else since our first dance." He loomed over me on braced arms and knees.

Knowing this would be probably the one and only time

I'd get a chance, I glided my fingers over his sculpted arms, pecs, and abs, feeling his muscles flex against my touch.

He closed his eyes, as if the caress of my fingertips was a balm to his soul. His reaction was the permission I needed to follow the pattern of the black-and-gray ink crisscrossing his body.

Some of his ink covered scars that I'd never learn the story behind.

Pushing the last thought back, I continued to explore this exquisite man.

"Harder. I want to feel your nails on my skin."

I followed his command, scoring my nails up and down his body, causing goosebumps to appear and a low rumble to erupt from his throat.

"Lower, Isa."

My eyes shifted down past his waist. The heavy press of his cock was a long, thick ridge along the inside of his pant leg. He couldn't be that big.

"Go ahead. I want you to feel the condition I've been in for the last five months."

I cupped him and gasped.

Nope, that was all him.

Was I really going to let him put this monster in me?

I rubbed up and down his length through his pants and stared into his dark eyes filled with heat and barely leashed control.

"I want you, Isa. I want you as I've never wanted a woman before. I want to bury myself in you and show you all the ways I can make you come."

Yes, I was definitely going to let him put it anywhere he wanted. If I didn't ever get to have this again, I'd have it tonight.

My face must have shown my thoughts because he cupped my jaw and said, "I don't want you to think of anything else but what's happening here. The world outside doesn't exist."

When I didn't respond, his grip tightened, and my heart skipped a beat. "Do you understand?"

The demand in his words sent a shot of arousal coursing through me. He'd just shown me a small taste of the dominant man, but until now, I hadn't realized he was holding back. I wanted to see all of it, but I wasn't sure he would ever reveal that part to me, or if I could ever let him go if he did.

I'd been so angry with him that day in the bar when he'd tried to get me to see what I wanted, and now all I cared about was getting to experience everything, at least this one time.

"Yes, I understand," I whispered.

"Now open my slacks and take me out."

I swallowed, released my hold on his cock, and worked open the button and zipper. He didn't help me, just continued to hold himself over me. I pushed his pants past his hips and down his perfect ass. His cock sprang free, hitting his stomach. A bead of precum dripped from the tip.

Holy fuck.

I was definitely going to be sore tomorrow.

"Frightened?" The way he said it told me he knew damn well he was hung, with both girth and length.

"No. I want this. I want to feel you with every step I take."

A feral gleam entered his eyes.

"Then I better make sure I deliver. Now finish undressing me."

But instead of listening, I reached down and collected the precum from the head of his beautiful cock. Bringing it to my lips, I licked and then hummed.

"As much as I'd love to have you climb over me and suck my cock until I come, I want to sink inside your tight pussy. Take off my clothes, Isa."

"I'm at a bit of a disadvantage to accomplish your instructions with you caging me."

"You can figure it out."

I lifted my legs, letting my toes hook his belt loops and pull the fabric down to his knees.

A slight curve of his lips told me he hadn't expected my approach.

"You never cease to surprise me." He pushed his pants the rest of the way off. "You're like no other woman I've ever met. I really hope you won't hate me in the future."

Why would I hate him? For making me want him? Never.

I cupped his face. "Just you and me here. Nothing else."

"Isa," he moaned and covered my lips again.

His hard body came down over mine. The light dusting of hair on his chest grazed my nipples, making them strain tighter and ache. Lifting my hips, I rubbed my clit against the hard ridge of his length.

His tongue slid and rolled against mine, filling me with his intoxicating taste. I clutched his hair as my other hand held on to his shoulder.

Wrapping my legs around his waist, I arched against him, reveling in the sensation of his cock pressed along my soaked opening. He rolled his pelvis, torturing me with need.

Breaking the kiss, I gasped in air and said, "I want you in me. Please."

"Only you would beg and demand at the same time."

"Bazzz," I whined.

He lifted up and grabbed a condom sitting on the side table.

When had he put that there?

He tore the foil package and sheathed his cock. I watched him stroke up and down, making my mouth water for a taste.

"I'm making you mine, Isa. No man will ever give you what I will."

I reached for him and he climbed between my spread legs. But instead of aligning his cock and driving in, he bent down, covering my clit with his mouth and pushing two fingers into my pussy.

"Oh God," I cried out as my back bowed.

He worked my pussy with his fingers, tongue and mouth, bringing me to the cusp of release before easing back.

He repeated the sadistic torture two more times.

"No more, Baz. I beg you. Let me come."

"Soon." He slid up my body but kept his fingers buried deep in me, continuing to pump in and out.

When I was about to scream, he pulled free, bringing his fingers to my mouth.

"Suck."

I stared at his hand for a brief moment and then opened my lips, sucking my essence from him.

He reached down, grabbing hold of his thick cock and sliding it up and down my dripping slit. My heart beat into my ears and my need grew.

"Please."

"You're mine, Isa. No matter what happens, you're mine."

The truth of what he was saying hit me. I'd never belonged to any other man the way I belonged to him. He was mine too.

"Say it, Isa." The bulbous head of his cock breached the opening of my pussy. "Give me the words."

Sweat beaded his forehead, revealing the restraint he was holding on to.

"I'm yours. I belong to you. No one else."

"Forever." He pushed in farther. "Say it."

"Forever," I moaned at the same moment he slammed all the way in.

We both cried out together.

I felt full, nothing like I'd experienced before. He

throbbed inside me, unmoving even though I knew he wanted to. He was so big, almost too big.

"Breathe, baby. Relax."

The soft crooning of his deep voice calmed something in me and caused my muscles to relax.

"I'm okay." Threading my fingers into his hair, I brought him down for a kiss and then murmured, "I need you to move now."

"I'm happy to oblige."

He began with shallow thrusts, letting me become accustomed to his size. My body responded, growing slicker, easing his glide in and out. The second I squirmed under him, his movements grew harder and more forceful.

"Yes. Like that." I was lost in the cascade of sensation; my pussy quickened and clamped around his pistoning cock.

"Baz. Oh God. Baz."

"That's it, *Prinzessin*. Let go."

My fingernails scored down his back as the first pulse of my orgasm hit me.

I heard Baz hiss and then his cock grew harder, if that was possible.

He grabbed hold of my arms, pinning them above my head. He dropped his forehead to mine and stared into my eyes.

"If you keep doing that, I'll come and I'm not ready for that. I need to feel you shatter at least twice before that happens."

The only thing I could say in response was, "Okay."

We spoke no more words, just let our bodies take over. I was lost in him, lost in his kiss, the feel of him on me and in me.

He held on to my arms, controlling my response, and when I shattered, it was like falling over a cliff, exhilaration and fear. My pussy spasmed and clenched around him, and my mind clouded with a level of pleasure I knew I'd only ever experience in this man's arms.

"That's it, love. Now give me one more."

He continued to pound into me, not letting me come down from my high. My body continued to glide until I erupted again, but this time bringing him with me.

He came as hard as I did, calling out, "Mine, mine, mine."

I closed my eyes at the emotion his declaration brought out and knew I'd never be the same again.

CHAPTER NINE

I woke to the feel of lips on my shoulder.

"Baz," I moaned, curling into his heat.

"Sleep, baby. I'm going to make a few calls and then we need to talk."

"What time is it?"

"A little after four."

It had only been about an hour since we'd fallen asleep following a marathon sex session.

"You work in the middle of the night?"

"I work at all hours of the night." He kissed my shoulder and then ran his fingers down my spine. "When I get back, I plan to bury myself deep in you again. I promised to make you feel me with every step you take."

That was definitely a given. I ached, but in the best way.

"I'm holding you to it." I yawned into my pillow.

Baz chuckled, leaving me in his bed.

Last night had been so much more than I expected. I'd

never had a man make me come as hard as Baz had or do any of the things he'd done to me.

I'd let him bind me, spank me, fuck me.

I hadn't expected to wake after our first round of sex with my hands tied to the top of the bed.

"You're bound, baby. I'm about to show you what it means to give up complete control."

Those heated words he'd said even now had my heartbeat accelerating and my core contracting.

He'd definitely done as he'd promised. Now dawn was almost upon us.

Every time I thought about the daylight ending my time with Baz, sadness filled my heart.

In a few hours, I'd leave for my family's home on the coast and a wedding to a man I barely knew anything about, and my night with Baz would be a cherished memory.

Might as well get up and spend every moment I had left with him. I slipped from the bed, grabbing Baz's shirt from a chair in a corner. I slipped it on and knotted my hair into a loose bun.

I opened the door to find the hallway empty. Padding my way toward the living room, I found myself pausing outside a closed door. I heard a loud discussion. Baz sounded annoyed.

Just as I was about to walk away, I heard, "Are you fucking kidding me, Weber? Just because you're getting married doesn't mean you don't finish your paperwork. I have enough shit to deal with after losing your partner to matrimony. Do you know how hard it's going to be to train another American the way we run things?"

Weber?

"Stop bitching, old man. It's already filed. I took care of it. Besides, I have my own problems."

"I heard. How are you going to break it to your bride that you've spent the last few months lying to her?"

"Fuck off. I was planning to come clean, but your ass wants a report."

All the blood drained from my face and a wave of nausea hit me.

Baz was a Weber. As in, Sebastian Weber.

No, this couldn't be. He wouldn't do this to me. I'd been honest with him from the beginning.

"Look, once we close this, you can spend the next few months groveling." The voice on the other line laughed. "I wish I had a camera to record the infallible Sebastian Weber grovel."

It was him.

He'd tricked me. He'd used me.

I braced my hand on the wall trying to understand why he'd do this.

It made no sense.

Was this some sick way to make me fall for him? God, who had I fallen for?

A tear spilled down my cheek.

How could I have let this happen? I should have known something was up when he'd shown up at the bar that day in my parents' neighborhood. I remembered *Oma* saying my fiancé had just left.

That was the business he had.

God, I was such an idiot.

I'd let him use me.

He was exactly like his father.

Turning, I went into Baz's...*Sebastian's* bedroom. The room smelled of us, our lovemaking, of him.

How could he do this to me?

I grabbed my clothes piled on the floor and put them on. By the time I was dressed, hurt and anger pulsed inside me.

I had no choice but to go through with this, but I'd never give him again what he'd stolen from me.

I wiped away my tears as I made my way into the living room and to the front door, making sure to keep my steps quiet.

I was no longer Baz's lover. Starting from this point on, I was the prize bought by the Webers.

P resent Day
　　Sebastian

"Y ou're so fucked," I heard my best man, Lucas Flynn, whisper as the music shifted into the wedding march.

I ignored him and stared at Isa. She was beyond gorgeous, beyond anything I deserved. She wore a fitted gown of ivory without a veil. It fitted her personality: modern, simple, and stylish, no trace of what one would expect of the daughter of one of the richest men in Germany.

I was about to bring her into a world that could destroy not only my family, but hers. But I was a bastard, and instead of telling Jonas to fuck himself, I was taking the empire and the woman that came with it.

The passion and joy I'd seen every time Isa looked at me was gone, replaced by anger and hurt.

The hard edge to Russo Benz's face said he wasn't any happier about this wedding than his daughter was.

The moment he placed Isa's hand in mine, he said, "I don't care who you are or what you do. If you hurt my baby, I will tear you limb from limb."

I didn't respond, just led Isa to the altar.

The ceremony went by in a blur of vows, rings, and prayers. The latter being something I felt was sacrilegious considering the business both families engaged in.

"You may kiss your bride."

Isa and I gazed at each other before I cupped her face and drew her to me. The kiss was gentle and soft, but cold, with none of the passion we'd shared a week ago.

"Isa," I whispered. "I'm sorry."

She said nothing, only gave me a slight smile, meant for the photographer who hovered near us.

She turned to face the church as did I when the crowd stood and clapped.

We moved down the aisle and toward the holding room. We would wait there until security had cleared the church and my driver arrived with the car. I knew Isa had been briefed about protocol.

The second we entered the secured room, Isa shoved me back.

Fury blazed on her face. "How could you? You made me… You let me believe… I'll never forgive you."

"Please, Isa, let me explain." I reached for her, but she stepped back.

"No, you had your chance. You had plenty of chances. It wasn't as if I wasn't going to marry you." The tears glazing her eyes were like a stab in the heart. "I don't even know if everything that happened between us was real or if it was all a game. What I do know is that I will never give you again what you stole."

Before she could move farther away from me, I grabbed her arm, stopping her escape from me.

"What you saw was the real me, not Jonas Weber's son or the man the public believes I am. Everything I shared with you was the truth."

"Bullshit." She clenched her jaw and tugged her wrist, but my grip was too strong for her to free herself.

"It's not bullshit. You know more about me than anyone else."

"If that's true, then why is your name Sebastian? You told me it was Baz Klein."

Her blue eyes blazed with anger, and her breath was uneven from struggling to pull free of my hold.

She was so damn beautiful, and all I wanted to do was haul her to me and kiss her senseless.

"No answers," she bit out.

"It is Baz. Baz was the nickname my mother gave me when I was a kid. No one has called me by that name since she died. And Klein was her maiden name."

Surprise flashed in her cobalt gaze then disappeared. "It doesn't matter what your name is. You lied to me."

"I didn't lie to you. I just kept things from you."

My answer sounded lame even to my own ears.

"Not telling me the truth of who you are is just like lying."

"I'm sorry, baby."

"I'm not your baby. I'm the prize my mother sold to yours."

"You're more than that. I swear I was going to tell you."

"When? After you spent the night fucking me and pretending to be another man?"

"I was going to tell you in the morning, but when I came back to the bedroom, you were gone."

"What did you expect? I overheard your conversation."

Fuck. I ran a hand through my hair. She wasn't supposed to know anything about that aspect of my life. No one in my world as Sebastian Weber knew.

I was just building up all the lies.

Before I could respond, the doors opened and I released Isa.

Drew, my driver, peeked his head in. His gaze went between Isa and me. There was no doubt we were in a heated argument, but he kept his reaction schooled.

"Mr. Weber, the car is out front and ready to take you to the Benz house."

"We'll be there in a few minutes."

The door closed.

"We'll settle this once we get to the penthouse. Until then, you can hate me all you want. Just pretend to be accepting, if not happy. Your family needs to see you aren't angry."

"Why do you care how they feel? As of tomorrow morning, you're the heir to everything Papa built, and your father will get a big fat inheritance."

"Despite what you believe, I'm nothing like my father. He's a bastard who would have ruined my family if *Opa* hadn't ordered him to let me step in. I'm a victim of this mess as much as you are. I can only hope one day you'll see it."

I offered her my elbow. "Let's go. Our families are waiting."

CHAPTER TEN

Isa

Around one in the morning, Sebastian and I entered his penthouse in silence. Unlike the last time, I wasn't the idiot who'd fallen for a man who didn't exist.

The reception was a somber affair, with everyone on their best behavior. Well, with the exception of Jonas Weber. He'd sat at his table all smug and making jokes.

Sebastian hadn't looked at him twice. I hadn't realized how much Sebastian disliked Jonas. Maybe Sebastian was a victim of Jonas's scheming as I was. That still didn't give him the excuse to lie to me, to pretend to be just an ordinary man.

Who was I kidding? The Baz I'd met was never an ordinary man. I wouldn't have been so interested if he had been.

"Do you want something to drink?" Sebastian asked as he shrugged off his tuxedo jacket, threw it on a sofa, and moved to the giant bar area that made up one wall of the room.

"No." I stepped down into the very modern sunken living room with straight lines and dark colors.

I hadn't paid attention to the room the last time I was here. I'd been too focused on the night ahead with Baz.

As I approached the windows overlooking the Berlin night sky, I heard the clinking of a bottle and the splash of liquid pouring into a glass.

After a few moments, Sebastian said, "Isa, I want this to work."

I almost laughed. "It's not like we can walk away if it doesn't work."

I couldn't hide the bitterness in my tone. Bitterness not for the marriage, but for feeling like a fool by falling for him.

"It matters to me. I don't want the type of marriage my parents had."

I'd heard rumors that Jonas was as much a bastard to his wife as he'd been to my family. He'd only valued her for the inheritance he'd gained by marrying her.

"You should've thought of that before you pretended to be someone else."

"I made a mistake. I should've stayed away or just told you from the beginning."

"It doesn't change what happened. You bought me. You own me. I'm your property."

"You know I don't believe in that shit."

I whirled around. "Do I? As far as I'm concerned, we just met."

"Dammit, Isa. I'm the same man."

"It doesn't matter. I know the rules. I give you my body in exchange for my family's livelihood."

"Is that really how you want it between us? A business arrangement?"

The last thing I wanted was to be in this situation, but Sebastian wasn't my Baz. Baz was a figment of my imagination.

Lilly had been right. I'd been played.

"Yes."

Sebastian clenched his jaw and ran a frustrated hand through his hair.

"Fine. If that's how you want it. I can be the bastard you believe me to be. Remember, I grew up with the number-one example."

"I expect nothing less."

He stalked toward me, and without thought I stepped backward. He was angry, but for some reason, I had no fear of him. In fact, I was aroused.

God, I was so messed up.

I was now married to one of the most dangerous men in Germany, a man who'd lied to me for months, a man who made me fall in love with a ghost, and here I was, turned on by his anger.

My back hit the window a second before he gripped my jaw in his hand.

I gasped, "Ba…Sebastian."

He leaned in until I felt the heat of his breath and smelled the faint scent of the whiskey he'd sipped. "You're mine now. As you said, I own you. And you want to know something?"

"What?" My voice came out breathy.

"I'm never letting you go."

His mouth came down on mine, and instead of biting him like my mind said to do, I met his kiss with my own. He was like a drug, one I knew was dangerous but couldn't resist.

He kept his grip on my face as he deepened the kiss, and my arms came around his shoulders. Our tongues dueled, rolling and sliding against each other. It was an angry, hungry meeting of mouths and lips.

His cock was thick and hard against my pelvis, causing a moan to escape my lips.

All of a sudden, he pulled back and broke the intense kiss, both of us breathless and panting. His eyes were near black and his face flushed.

Holding my gaze, he pulled his bowtie free, tucking it into the back pocket of his pants, and then unbuttoned his shirt, working the black stone buttons free until his breathtaking tattooed chest was exposed.

Shrugging off the white material, he threw it behind him to land on the couch.

He looked like a fallen angel, something forbidden but too tempting to resist.

My throat went dry and my breasts swelled, pushing

my nipples into tight, hard buds aching for his touch. My clit throbbed, and my pussy flooded with arousal.

"Turn around and put your hand on the glass." The tone of his voice was different, unlike anything I'd heard from him before.

It made me want to run and comply at the same time.

"Isa, now."

My body moved of its own volition, turning and pressing my fingertips to the cool window.

"What are you going to do?"

"You'll just have to find out."

"No spanking. You no longer have the right."

He fisted my hair and tugged it back, harder than he'd ever done before. "You can't say no. Remember, you're my property. I can do with you as I please."

He kicked my legs apart, pushing the fabric of my gown impossibly tight around my legs.

"Fuck, that ass of yours is incredible." Releasing my hair, he cupped my butt in a tight hold.

His almost painful hold conjured images of that night when he'd reddened my ass and the pleasure of it.

I shouldn't be letting him do this. I didn't trust him. I couldn't trust him.

Slowly he slid his palms up, over my bottom, waist, and breasts, cupping them and then pinching the tips through the embroidered top of my wedding dress.

"I hope you're not attached to this dress."

Before I could comprehend what he was doing, he

gripped the back where the zipper connected and tore the fabric in two.

I gasped and covered my breasts, pooling the material in front of me. Yes, I knew he'd seen every inch of me but this wasn't the same as when we were last together.

"Drop your hands. You'll never hide your body from me. I get to look at you whenever I want. Especially since you're my property." The emphasis he gave to the "property" part made it very clear he was pissed about how I'd referred to myself as that.

"What am I then?" I asked without dropping my hands.

He ran his fingertips up my spine, starting at the waistband of my thong. Goosebumps prickled my skin.

When he reached the base of my neck, his lips replaced his fingers, and I couldn't help but arch back into the caress.

"My wife, my woman, mine." His tongue followed the path his fingers had just taken.

"It's not that simple."

"Yes, it is. Lower your arms. Let the dress fall."

"What if someone sees us from the window?"

"It's tinted. I like my privacy. No one can see in. Now do as I said."

Closing my eyes, I let the ruined gown slip from my arms and pool at my feet.

"Now I'm going to make sure you keep those hands where I want them."

He captured my wrists before I could move, setting them above my head on the window. Then he wrapped my hands together with a black ribbon. No, it wasn't a ribbon, it was his bowtie.

My pulse jumped. These were things I fantasized about but never expected to act out.

The glint of the wedding band on his ring finger as he knotted the tie had me feeling the same sense of possessiveness he'd expressed moments earlier. I really was losing my mind around this man. How could I want to punch him and kiss him at the same time?

"Leave them there. If you move them. I will spank your ass and won't let you come."

"No spanking."

Immediately, I felt the sting of his palm against my ass.

"Fuck," I gasped.

He rubbed the sore spot. "Now tell me again that you don't want it. Tell me that your ass isn't craving more or pushing against my hand right now."

I froze, realizing I was seeking his stinging touch.

"I hate you."

"No, you don't. You're just angry the man you had an affair with is the man you ended up marrying."

I shot him an irritated glare. "No, I'm angry because the man I thought I knew turned out to be a fraud."

"Be angry all you want. You're still married to me and all the many faces I wear."

I almost asked what he meant by that statement when he moved the gusset of my thong and pressed a finger deep inside me.

"Oh God," I moaned, now pissed off at my own body and its need for this man.

"You're dripping." He pulled out and brought his fingers to my lips. "Suck."

"Aren't you afraid I'll bite you? I'm in a biting kind of mood."

He coated my lips with my essence. "Go ahead. Your ass will suffer the consequences. Now open."

I complied, letting the taste of my arousal explode on my tongue.

"Good?"

I nodded.

"Let me see if I agree." He clutched my hair, tugging my head back and covering my mouth with his.

The kiss was all-consuming and so different from what we'd shared before. It was as if, now that the truth was out, he wasn't going to hold back.

"Like ambrosia for the gods," he murmured as he pulled back. "I have one question for you."

"What?"

"Flogger or my hand?"

"You can't be serious. *No spanking.*"

"Then flogger, it is."

The idea of it had my insides heating but was I ready? The furthest I'd ventured into this world was what I'd experienced a week earlier and we'd done nothing more than spanking.

"I'm not sure."

We hadn't even figured out how this whole thing with

us was going to work. Hell, I was still so hurt and angry with him.

God, I was losing my mind.

"I saw your reaction to the scene at the club. I know you wanted to experience what Kiera was feeling. The one thing I'm very good at is reading people."

I dropped my head to the glass. "I promised myself I wouldn't let you take this part of me again."

He hands came around me, covering mine, and his hard chest pressed against my back. It was like being cocooned in his heat, in his strength.

"I'm not going to take anything. This is about you giving yourself to me, freely. You tell me you truly don't want it, then it won't happen."

I opened my mouth to say I wanted this to stop, to truly stop, but I couldn't get the words out of my mouth.

"If I say I don't want it, will you leave me alone?"

"Do you want me to?"

His delicious scent tickled my nose and my head fell back against his neck. "You confuse me. Why do I need you so much? I should hate you."

"But you don't. Now tell me, flogger or my hand. You need it as much as I do."

I inhaled deep, knowing there was no way I was stopping this. I wanted to feel the bite of the thin straps of the leather against my skin, and the painful pleasure that I'd seen Kiera experience.

"Flogger."

I felt his lips curve against my skin. "Good choice. Stay here. And that means don't move a muscle."

He lifted off me, and immediately I missed the feel of his heat, his hard body, his presence.

I couldn't believe I was really going to let him flog me after everything that had happened.

As Lilly would say to me, I was dickmatized. That was the only answer. One night of incredible sex had me craving more even when logic said I should fight him tooth and nail for lying to me.

After a few minutes, I felt myself growing restless.

Where the hell had he gone?

I turned my head to peek behind me and found him sitting on the arm of the sofa with the flogger in his hand. The way he looked reminded me of the Dom from the club, Liam. But unlike Liam, Baz had an aura around him that had my core clenching.

"Why are you sitting there?"

"I was waiting for you to work out all the turmoil in your head."

"That's not going to happen anytime soon."

He rose, stepping in my direction. "Then maybe this will help you forget for a while."

He placed a hand on my back, pressing my naked breast to the cool glass.

"I'll start with slow strokes, letting them grow harder until a light pink flush covers every inch of your exposed skin. The only way I'll stop is if you say a safe word. What's your safe word, Isa?"

We were really doing this.

I thought for a second and then said, "Deception."

I could almost hear him clench his jaw.

"Deception, it is. Let's begin."

I braced for the sting of the flogger but what came was the feel of his warm hands stroking my skin, over my calves, up my thighs, and all over my back.

The gentleness of his touch brought tears to my eyes. It was like he was memorizing every one of my curves.

I gasped when his lips grazed my lower spine.

This wasn't what I wanted. He was supposed to make me lose myself in the feel of the pain and the pleasure. He wasn't supposed to make me need him like this.

When his lips moved to the back of my neck, tingles shot through my body and my heart clenched.

Without realizing it, I whispered, "Deception."

Sebastian froze, turning my face to the side to look at him. "We haven't even started."

"I can't, not today when you're touching me like this. Like I mean something to you."

"You do mean something, Isa. You meant something to me from that moment our eyes connected in your club." He stared into my eyes. "What do you want to do? Stop completely?"

I didn't want to make this decision. I wanted him to make it for me, but that wasn't how this worked.

"I want you to fuck me, no kink, no making love. Just fucking. I don't want to think about anything but the feel of your cock in me."

A flash of hurt and pain passed through his dark eyes as he stepped back. Without another word, he pushed off his shoes and unbuttoned his pants, letting them drop to the floor, followed by his boxer briefs. His cock, thick and heavy, pointed upward.

He fisted the base with a tight grip, causing precum to drip from the tip.

The feral look in his eyes as he moved toward me and stroked his cock had my core spasming.

It was obvious we weren't going to use a condom. I'd never gone bare before, and the idea of it was both frightening and exciting.

This was my husband, a man who'd broken my heart, the man who'd father my children, the man who seemed to have possessed me into wanting him like no other person before.

He braced a hand over my bound wrists, pressing me onto the cool window and making my nipples pebble harder.

He slid the thick length of his cock down between my ass cheeks and through the slit of my pussy lips, stopping at my clit to rub the sensitive bundle of nerves with his bulbous head.

I couldn't hide my whimper.

"Do you want this?"

I didn't respond, and he repeated the delicious torture.

"I asked you a question."

"Y-y-yes."

"You want to stop thinking?"

"Yes."

"You want to feel my cock fucking into you?"

"Yes."

"Yes what?"

"Please," I begged.

I was going to go out of my mind.

"Wrong." He rimmed my pussy, pushing in a frustrating fraction of an inch. "The correct answer is yes, Baz."

I glared over my shoulder. "Yes, Sebastian."

"Wrong again." He thrust in a little farther and immediately pulled out.

I clenched my bound hands, dropping my forehead to the window. "I won't say it. You aren't my Baz."

He leaned in and bit the juncture of my shoulder and neck. "We're the same person. One is who I have to be, one is who I am with you."

I wanted to believe him.

"Say it, Isa."

A tear slipped down my cheek. "Baz."

He pushed in to the hilt.

"Say it again." He pulled out.

"Baz."

"That's right. I'm Baz." He began a relentless pace, pounding into me.

My pussy quivered, quickening in slow pulses.

"More. I need more."

"You'll take what I give you." He pressed his body flush against my back, leaving no room between his skin and mine. "You're mine, Isa."

He pulled out and thrust back in.

"I will take your control, but not tonight. I want you to know it's me who's fucking you. Not just any cock."

"Baz, please. Harder."

His pace quickened. "This is your husband fucking you. You'll never forget it."

His fingers slipped between me and the window, finding my clit and giving it a gentle stroke.

"Yes," I cried out as my body flew over the cliff in release.

My pussy clenched around his pistoning cock, soaking him in my juices.

"Fuck, fuck, fuck. I can't hold out any longer." Sebastian came in a loud roar, pumping me full of his cum.

CHAPTER ELEVEN

Sebastian

I tried to calm my breath and tame the pounding in my chest. I'd just had the most incredible orgasm of my life with the woman of my dreams. Now I had to figure a way out of the mess I'd created with her.

Reluctantly, I lifted my weight off Isa's back and pulled free of her snug pussy.

Fuck, I was still half hard.

No matter how much I wanted to fuck her nonstop, we had to talk.

"Let's get you cleaned up and in bed. We need to have a long conversation."

She stirred, raising her head from the glass.

"Is sex between us always going to be this intense?"

Hopefully this sex-drunk state of hers would open her

to listen to what I had to say. There were things I had to share with her and there were things I could never share with her. I hadn't lied when I said I wore many faces. I was the ruthless mobster the world believed me to be but I was also the man who used my position to stop and take down scum worse than myself.

"I have no doubt." I kissed her naked back as I untied her wrists and rubbed her arms as I brought them down.

She moaned. "I don't think I have the energy to walk."

"Well that's good. Then you're a captive audience for the discussion we're going to have." I scooped her into my arms, letting her burrow into my chest.

"I'm still mad at you."

"I wasn't expecting anything else. But I'm not the bastard you believe me to be."

She lifted her head and raised a brow.

"Okay, I *am* a bastard, but I have my reasons."

Carrying her into the bedroom, I laid her on the bed and felt my heart skip a beat.

She was a goddess with her kiss-swollen lips, tousled black hair, eyes so blue they looked artificial. I'd had my share of models, actresses, and socialites with polish and perfection but none held a candle to this woman.

My woman.

"I'll be back." I went into the bathroom, returning with a warm, damp washcloth and came down beside her.

As I cleaned the cum from between her legs, I felt my cock go from semi-hard to completely erect. I was constantly hard around her.

Her fingers wrapped around me, squeezing tight and making me hiss.

I tried to pull her hands from my cock. "We have to talk, Isa."

She wasn't deterred. "I don't want to talk. I want to fuck. We have the rest of our lives to talk."

I closed my eyes and threw back my head as she pumped up and down.

"Baby, I'm trying to fix the mess I created." My words came out in a plea.

God, this woman had me begging. I fucking never begged. Then again, I'd never been this way with any other woman.

I'd spent my life perfecting the image I'd created. It helped me stay on top of business and scare the shit out of anyone I was associated with. But this woman had me gentling.

Hell, I'd spent over five months going on coffee dates where I'd done nothing but talk to her.

She'd had me in a state of perpetual blue balls.

"I don't want to fix it right now. I want as much angry sex as I can get." She pushed at my chest until I was on my back.

"Dammit, Isa. I'm trying to do the right thing."

Fury flashed in her cobalt gaze as she climbed over me. "A little late for that. Right now, I want the privileges of the body I got when I was sold to you."

I fisted her hair as my temper grew to match hers. "I

didn't buy you. I had no choice either. I was in college in America when this whole thing was negotiated."

All of a sudden, she broke my hold, pinning my hands back.

I couldn't hide my surprise as she loomed over me, the lips of her cunt positioned over the length of my straining cock.

"I said," she bit out, "I want to fuck." She slid up and down me, coating me with her arousal.

I knew a losing battle when I was in one.

"Keep your hands here."

"Is this a game of tit for tat?"

"Call it what you want. I want to enjoy this body that belongs to me."

The last thing I expected was to hear the possessiveness in her voice. If she believed she owned me, then far be it for me to argue.

"Go right ahead and claim me."

She brought her face to mine. "No talking."

She kissed me and then trailed her mouth down my neck, over my collarbone, and lower. When her tongue circled my sensitive nipples, I bucked up.

"Too much, baby. Too much."

She lifted her head. "I haven't even begun to torture you."

There was a wicked curve to her lips that had my dick oozing precum onto my stomach. If she kept this up, I was going to come like a fucking teenager.

She moved farther down, tracing and kissing my chest and abs.

I closed my eyes when her pussy slid lower and her lips were a hairsbreadth from my cock.

She gripped the base and licked around the engorged head, humming with each stroke of her tongue.

I shuddered as she continued to tease me.

"Tighter, squeeze me tighter," I ordered, loving the feel of her touch.

She followed my command, not taking exception as I expected her to. I grew harder in her hands and felt the urge to take over churning at the back of my mind.

"Suck me, Isa. Take me deep into your mouth."

My words caused a whimper from her lush lips and she lowered. Without thinking, I brought my hands down to clench her hair. God, I loved this wild mane of hair.

She took me in slowly, working up and down until I felt my cock hit the back of her throat. And then she did something that had me ready to lose my mind. She swallowed, contracting that incredible mouth.

"Isa. Do that again. Fuck. Do it again."

She worked me hard. The erotic and oh-so-sweet suction of her mouth more intense then I'd ever experienced.

I opened my eyes to lock with her blue ones, filled with pleasure and smug satisfaction.

She pumped her fist up and down with the tempo of her incredible mouth and tongue.

My balls drew up, and I knew I was about to lose all control.

"Isa, stop now or I'm going to come down your throat."

I almost thought she was going to ignore me and let me lose myself in her mouth, but she released me with a pop and a mischievous smile.

She crawled over me until her cunt hovered over my cock. She was an incredible sight, lips swollen and wet from sucking me and face flushed.

"I'm going to fuck you now, Sebastian."

I narrowed my gaze, lifting up until I was sitting and grabbing hold of her hips. "The only man you will ever fuck again is Baz."

She met my challenge with her own. "You haven't earned the right to be my Baz."

"Believe what you want. I'm never going to be anyone else. Not with you, anyway."

I lifted her and then lowered her, engulfing my cock in her liquid heat.

A moan escaped her lips and her head fell back, making her breath come out in soft pants.

"Christ, you feel incredible." Sliding my hands up her body, I cupped her perfect breasts, teasing the taut buds until they grew harder.

"Ride me, baby."

Her arms came around my shoulders and she rose, using her knees, and lowered in a slow, languid slide, gyrating her hips in a way that was meant to drive me insane.

"Isa," I groaned, loving the way her pussy clutched my cock with every movement.

I lowered my head, sucking one delicious nipple into my mouth.

"Oh God," she moaned and continued to strangle my cock with her slow rise and fall. "This feels so good."

"Yes, it does. You're so wet. Your juices are soaking me."

Her rhythm grew faster, harder, and I knew she was about to go over.

Sliding my thumb toward her clit, I pressed down. Immediately, her cunt quivered and her breath grew unsteady.

"Come, my love. Come hard on my cock."

As if she'd been waiting for my command, she came, detonating, squeezing me so tight I saw stars, and pushing me into my own release.

A little after ten in the morning, I walked into my childhood home knowing I was about to do the one thing I'd dreamed of since I was a small boy.

Kick Jonas Weber out of the family home and business. As of midnight, while I was buried deep in my wife, one hundred percent of Weber International had become mine. No more dealing with him holding the company or my responsibilities over my head. No more waiting for the day the bastard who was a father to me in name only could lord his presence over me. The hierarchy had shifted, and now I was the man at the helm.

With the change in power, it also meant I had to keep an even closer eye on Jonas. It wouldn't matter that the deal was executed and he'd inherited an exorbitantly funded trust as a retired family head, he would want more —nothing was ever enough for the man. It wouldn't surprise me if Jonas blew through all the money by the end of five years, probably sooner.

Lucas met me at the entrance.

"You ready?" He handed me the paperwork I knew Jonas wasn't expecting.

"I've waited my whole life for this."

The bastard truly believed I'd take his word about the contracts *Opa* had signed at face value. *Opa* wasn't a stupid man and he was well aware what Jonas was like. Of *Opa*'s three sons, Jonas was the most spoiled, the most entitled. Andrew had been raised to take over as head and knew his responsibilities. And Fredrik, my only other living relative, was as mild-mannered as they came. *Opa* had known his youngest son wasn't meant for the lifestyle and allowed him to leave Germany and become a professor of economics in the United States.

Fredrik was a good man and deserved to live a life free of our family's taint. Because of this, I'd pushed him to leave Germany the minute the wedding reception was over. The fact my uncle had readily agreed told me Fredrik suspected his older brother was going to do something.

And the second I gave Jonas his orders, he'd become my

most dangerous adversary. Someone I couldn't turn my back on.

"He's not alone." Lucas shrugged. "It's his weekly Sunday booty call day. Some people go to church on Sunday mornings, he gets a blow job. At least this girl is legal. Well, I hope she is."

It made my stomach roll thinking Jonas took children to bed. I wanted to give him the benefit of the doubt that he only liked them to look young, but then again, he was a sick bastard.

If I ever got proof he was taking children to bed, I would kill him myself. After my last assignment, any man who thought to pursue that line of entertainment was a dead man in my book.

"The sooner that piece of shit is out of here, the sooner I'm free of him."

"That's harsh. Not even going to let him blow his load before he's out on the street."

"Asshole," I muttered, moving in the direction of Jonas's office.

I gestured to the soldiers positioned around the first floor of the house to follow me. Each of them had been part of our family's organizational structure since we were children, many of whom came from generations of service to the Webers. They were well aware the power structure had shifted and their loyalty was to the head of the family.

I stopped outside Jonas's office doors. "Let's get this over with. I have a wife to get back to."

As I gripped the handle, Lucas said, "No luck in taming her temper?"

I thought back to the angry sex we'd had all night long and how I'd woken to an empty bed and apartment.

"Not even close."

At least she'd left a note saying she'd taken her security to work and that she was under no circumstances giving up her clubs.

I'd have smiled at her words if I wasn't so irritated to have slept through her leaving. It wasn't like me to not notice the slightest movement or sound in a room.

"You look like a man well-fucked, so at least she didn't cut off your dick."

I glared at Lucas and opened the door.

"What the fuck?" Jonas roared while he pushed the helpless woman who was on her knees to the side.

How the hell I was related to this ass was a wonder to me. He was more cliché than a mobster movie.

"It's time to evict you from the property." The last thing I wanted to see was his dick hanging out of his pants. "Might want to put that away, wouldn't want anyone to get the wrong idea."

"I fucking live here."

"No. You *lived* here. As of midnight, this house, all of its contents and everything under Weber International belongs to me, Sebastian Alexander Weber."

"Bullshit. I know what the contracts say. I keep the house."

"Wrong. You should try reading the fine print instead of

believing everything your lawyers say. The Benz family keeps all its holdings and properties until Russo passes. You, on the other hand, get nothing but the trust set aside once the contract is executed." I glanced at the woman who was in tears trying to hide herself behind Jonas's chair. "You can leave. One of my men will make sure you get home. Next time think better of getting involved with old men who are only going to use you."

The woman ran from the room, ready to escape the chaos.

Jonas's face was beet red now. At least he'd had the decency to pull up his pants. "Do you understand who I am? With one word, I can have you eliminated."

"Go right ahead. I dare you. You'll learn very quickly the only reason the soldiers stayed with the organization was because their loyalty was to the family, not you."

"I think you'll see that things don't work the way you think. You're just like your *Opa*. You have no idea how to move with the times. You'll learn sooner rather than later that my methods of business are the way to go." He walked around me, as if he were a king about to leave. "Don't expect me to help you when things go to shit."

"I won't." As Jonas went to the door, I said, "Also, the contract says if you do anything to undermine the family, all monies in the trust revert to the heir. Don't think to mess with me, my business, or my wife." I added the last part to emphasize that I knew how he'd treated her.

"Boy, don't make an enemy of me. You won't like the outcome."

I kept my face emotionless, the best way to piss him off. I'd heard this over and over since I was old enough to understand the business my family was in.

Opa had always said power either made the man or destroyed the man. In Jonas's case, it was the latter, but he wasn't aware of it. Soon he would see without the Weber organization behind him, his millions would make him no different than any other man in Europe with too much money and no clout.

"Is that a threat?"

Immediately the room grew silent; the soldiers watched Jonas as if he were ready to pull a gun on me. All of them had heard about what he'd done when he'd informed me about the wedding.

As if sensing the change in loyalty with the Weber guard, he said, "It's a warning." And then strode through the door.

The moment he was out of view, I nodded to Lucas, who followed Jonas to make sure the asshole didn't take anything that could cause me problems in the future.

The bastard was officially evicted.

Destroying Jonas had been my ultimate goal ever since Mama and Hannah were murdered. Jonas forcing me to marry Isa moved up the timetable, but things weren't as simple as taking over. Now I had to set up all the pieces for the dominoes to fall.

"Search every inch of this house, especially this room and his private quarters. I want to know anything and everything he's up to. Also scan for cameras and bugs. I wouldn't put it past him to record everything that went on in this house."

"Done." Emil, one of the lieutenants in charge of the house, went to a cabinet and pulled it free of the wall, exposing a safe. "I saw it a few years ago."

"Open it." I moved toward the steel door.

Emil pulled out his phone and called someone and then said, "Kurt will be here in a moment."

Kurt was a technology and security expert in the organization. I would have recruited him for other aspects of my world if I wasn't positive he would never leave the family.

Kurt arrived a minute later with a box. He pulled out wires and a square device of some type, attached it to the safe, and then typed in a code. The electronic safe lit up, and within a few seconds, beeped and opened.

I moved in. The safe was filled with stacks of folders. I pulled out the papers, setting them in a bag Emil had brought for me. Behind the folders I found a thumb drive and photographs of Isa, of her coming out of the gym, of her visiting her friends.

The last few had my blood going cold. The images showed Isa and me meeting for coffee, us at my club, her leaving my building the week before, her eyes haunted and full of sadness.

The bastard had known about us.

It wasn't like him to keep anything close to his chest. He loved to brag, to share his grand plans with the world.

There had to be something I was missing. Why hadn't

he used the photos to call me out to Isa? What was he trying to gain?

"Bring me a secure computer," I ordered, to no one in particular.

Kurt pulled one out, setting it in front of me. I attached the thumb drive.

As the contents appeared, I resisted the urge to throw the laptop across the room. There was nothing but spreadsheet after spreadsheet filled with details of officials across Europe who owed the family loyalty for favors rendered.

This list, however useful for the organization, did nothing to explain why Jonas was having Isa followed.

At that moment, Lucas appeared in the office.

"Where is he?" I asked, not looking up from the computer.

"Gone. He didn't even bother going back to his room. He had this smug look on his face as he walked out the door." Lucas came up beside me and picked up the pictures of Isa. "That bastard is up to something, and I believe you just handed him your Achilles heel."

I stared at the picture of me watching Isa as she watched the scene at the club. A blind man would have seen I was gone for her.

This was bad, very bad. And now I had to find a way to protect my pissed-off-to-holy-hell woman without clipping her wings.

CHAPTER TWELVE

<hr>

Isa

"Are you seriously at work the day after your wedding?" Lilly stated after slamming open my office door and plopping down on a chaise I had in the back of my office. "I distinctly remember you setting up a schedule so you could take a honeymoon or something."

"Good morning to you. And thanks for just walking in. I'm working on projections and budgets. And you know I get crabby when I have to deal with budgets."

Lilly ignored me and handed me a cup of coffee and a bag that I knew held my favorite pastries.

"First of all, I'm your best friend and business partner, I can walk in whenever I want. Second, your staff was freaked out at your seven a.m. appearance and called me to make sure you were okay. Thirdly, most people spend the nights and days after their wedding banging the headboard." All of a sudden, Lilly sat up. "Please tell me you didn't kill your new husband. Even your crazy connections won't get you out of that."

I almost laughed at her worry.

Lilly had been the one I'd run to after I'd discovered who Baz really was. She'd followed proper best-friend protocol and helped me plot Baz's painful demise. Then she'd calmed me down and got me to realize that I'd have the rest of our lives to make Baz pay for lying to me.

"No, he isn't dead."

"And?"

"And what?"

She growled. "You're so annoying. It's like pulling teeth to get a straight answer out of you."

"I'm not the one who didn't tell me her boyfriend worked for my future husband."

"You're never going to let it go, are you? I didn't know because I didn't ask. And Kane likes his head on his shoulders, so he never talks about the people he works for. Now answer my question."

"Was there a question in all that just came out of your mouth?"

"I swear, you make me want to pull out that gun you have hidden in your purse and shoot you."

I smiled at her. "It's not like you don't have one of your own."

"I feel it would be justice if I used yours."

We glared at each other and then burst into laughter.

I loved this woman. Somehow, she always knew the right way to get me to relax.

Once we were in a semblance of control, she asked, "How did last night go? I couldn't get anywhere near you after the wedding. It was as if Jonas Weber was making it clear to the world that you were a Weber now and not a Benz."

I wanted to agree but I'd been so lost in my anger for most of the reception, I hadn't even paid attention to Jonas. Well, except for when I overheard Sebastian tell Jonas to rein it in.

"What part of last night, in particular?" I knew where she was going with the question but I wasn't going to make it easy for her.

Plus, how was I supposed to tell her that I angry-fucked my husband's brains out but never really spoke to him?

"I should have known subtlety was never going to work with you. Did you sleep together?"

My cheeks heated. "You could say we slept periodically during the course of the night."

"Oh my God. You fucked like rabbits." Lilly tilted her head. "And why are you here right now and not continuing the marathon sex with your hot-as-sin husband? By the way, the man fills out a tux like no one else."

Yeah, he had looked good yesterday. Heart-stopping was a more accurate word. If there was ever a man who was born to wear a suit, it was Sebastian. Then there was the slight hint of the tattoos hidden under the designer tux. They made my hormones fire every time I saw them.

"Because I'm still not sure where we stand. I don't understand why he lied to me."

"I'm going to tell you this as your best friend." Lilly came around my desk, pushed my chair back, and then leaned down. "You need to get over it. No matter what, the two of you are till death do you part. There is no divorce in our world. Listen to his reasons, make him grovel, and make lots of babies to take over the Benz-Weber empire."

"I wish it were that easy. I'm still so hurt."

"Well, nothing is going to get resolved if you sneak out of your twenty-million-Euro penthouse and don't talk to him. I don't want you to end up a bitter, constantly pissed-off, cliché mob wife."

I rolled my eyes and failed at holding in the smile from the image she'd conjured. Lilly loved her American reality shows, especially the ones revolving around the mob and their families.

"I hear you. I promise, next time I see him, I'll give him a chance to clear the air."

"That's all I ask."

"It doesn't mean I'll get over it. But I'll listen."

"Maybe you can get some diamonds out of it. That's what my mom does, and Papa is your dad's second without the Weber bank account."

Lilly's father was a lieutenant in Papa's organization and made a healthy living, so I had no doubt he had enough to shower his wife with jewels. He also adored his wife and never wanted to be out of her good graces.

"I'm not a diamonds kind of girl."

"Then get him to buy you a long-range rifle." She frowned. "You're the only woman I know who'd get wet from a gift of a deadly weapon."

Very few people knew I had a thing for guns, especially sniper rifles. I'd taken lessons after my first job working for Solon. Then, when I'd moved on to helping with cases for other security agencies, I thought it was better to become proficient in all manner of guns and self-protection.

I shrugged. "Some of us have higher standards than others."

"Good to know." Sebastian's deep voice came from the door.

"Ba...Sebastian."

He narrowed his gaze. "I woke up alone."

His intense attention had desire prickling up my skin.

"I left you a note. Besides, didn't you have work to do yourself? I heard your man, Lucas, mention something at our reception."

Lucas was one of the few people from the Weber camp I'd met yesterday who I liked. I'd deduced he was Sebastian's second and was very protective of him.

"My work could have held until after breakfast." The heat in his eyes told me it wasn't food he was talking about.

"On that note, I'm out of here." Lilly scooted around me and moved toward the door, pausing when she reached Sebastian. "I'm serious, buy her a gun and all your worries are over."

"I appreciate the insight into my bride." His lips curved

in that wicked way that made butterflies enter my stomach.

Lilly wasn't immune to the smile either and flushed before rushing out the door.

"I like her. She has this energy that most people in our world don't."

His assessment of Lilly melted some of the ice I was holding between us.

"Lilly sees the world in color. She is the ultimate free-thinking, artsy girl. She is smart as they come and can be a shark when it comes to art and sculpture authentication but everything she does is with joy."

"It's good to have people who bring light into the world we live in." He shut the door, locking it, and then moved in my direction.

"What are you doing?" I tried to roll my chair back toward my desk, but he stopped my movement with a foot by one of the rollers.

"I'm following Lilly's advice and am about to grovel." He kneeled in front of me. "And then..."

I swallowed. "And then what?"

"And then we get to the making-babies part."

"What makes you think I'm not on birth control?"

He gripped the handles of my chair and shifted me to face him. "Because I had you investigated. I know everything there is to know about you."

"Sounds a bit stalkerish."

He shrugged. "It's what I do. Plus, it made sense since I was ordered to marry you."

"Wouldn't it be prudent for me to have the same level of information?"

"Go ahead, investigate me."

"I have. You're a ghost. I bet the little that's available about the all-powerful Sebastian Weber was strategically placed by you."

"As of this morning, the same applies to you."

I couldn't hide the surprise on my face. "Why would you do that?"

"Because the moment we spoke our vows, you were Eloisa Weber."

"What does that mean?"

"It means I will go to any lengths to protect what's mine." He leaned in until our foreheads touched. "In case there's any doubt, you are mine. You've been mine since that moment our eyes connected across the dance floor."

I pulled back. "I won't let you cage me. I've spent my whole life finding ways around the box my parents put me in. I won't do it anymore."

"The last thing I want to do is cage you. I won't force you to fit into a mold that isn't yours. However…" He paused, as if working through his words, and then spoke. "I will protect you in any way I see fit. I have many faces, and some of them are dark and make enemies. If anything happened to you, I'd turn the world upside down."

"I don't understand. We've only known each other for a few months."

"There are no lengths I wouldn't go for those I love."

My heart skipped a beat at his words and the intensity

of his onyx gaze. It was time to ask him about the deception of the past few months.

"Why did you lie to me?"

He shook his head. "Because I'm an idiot. I'd just gotten back from a business trip that didn't go as planned and my head wasn't on straight. I was pissed about our marriage and about the mess Jonas had created in my life. I decided to see the princess of the Benz empire in action."

"What did you learn?"

"On paper you seemed to be the opposite of what I expected. And then in person, you blew me away. Our attraction was instantaneous, but the connection that came along with it was even more staggering."

"You could've come clean that night. It would have been a relief to know I was compatible with my betrothed." I rolled my eyes at the term.

"I liked that you didn't know me as anything other than as Baz. I was a mystery to you and you got to know the real me, not the one I have to be as the Weber heir. Plus, the fact that you kept pushing me away for a man you never met had me wanting you even more."

"And knowing I was pushing you away for my fiancé, who happened to be you, didn't get you off at all," I added without any inflection to my words.

He grinned in a way that made me want to kiss him. He looked younger than his almost thirty years, like a little boy who was caught doing something he shouldn't.

"That did add to the challenge."

"So, does it mean that cheating on you with you is acceptable?"

He pulled my chair closer to him, pushing my jean-clad legs apart and letting his thighs settle in between them.

"If roleplay appeals to you, I have no problem with it." He cupped my cheek. "Just know that it's Baz who's under anything I play."

He'd spoken of roles and faces so much that until right now, I hadn't realized the toll being the Weber heir and now head of the family had taken on him.

I'd learned from Papa there was no room for weakness, or someone else would be ready to muscle into leadership.

Sebastian had shown me a side of himself that he never exposed to anyone.

Instead of responding, I turned my face into his palm. He ran a thumb gently over my lips.

"Does this mean I'm forgiven?"

I grinned. "Yes, but I reserve the right to bring it up whenever I feel like it. Especially when you piss me off."

"Then I guess I better do my best to stay in your good graces." He lifted my face for a light peck. "How about if I start with a few orgasms to help with the stress of running a business?"

S ebastian

. . .

I stared into Isa's blue eyes, which were filled with shock and interest.

"You can't be serious. Here? Anyone could disturb us."

"Here." I skimmed my fingers down her body until I reached the button of her jeans. "The next time you sit in this chair, I want you to imagine orgasming with my face buried in your cunt."

She licked her plump lips. "I'm not sure this is a good idea."

The desire on her face was a sharp contrast to her words.

"I believe it's the perfect idea."

Popping the fastening, I lowered the zipper and tugged the denim down. "Lift up."

She tilted her hips, and I bunched her pants around her heeled boots. Her shoes made her long legs look longer. They were definitely staying on.

"Hold the armrest and don't let go. If you do, I'll stop and you won't get to come until tonight when I'm deep in your wet pussy."

Fire heated her cobalt gaze as if she was ready to argue but she set her palms on the soft leather.

"Good girl."

"I'm only complying because you owe me many an orgasm for lying to me."

"Keep telling yourself that. I know the truth."

She was the type of woman who loved her control but when she relinquished it, that was when she was happiest.

The night before the truth came out, she'd trusted me in a way I'd never forget. I'd pushed her to explore her sexuality and she'd lost herself in the pleasure. Last night was a sharp contrast. Control was something she resisted giving up. It was a battle between her anger and her desire.

I gripped her waist, adjusting her so I'd have access to the honey that was her pussy.

"Are you ready?"

Her lips parted and her breath came out in short pants. "Yes."

I lowered my mouth to her exposed belly button, rubbing my lips and jaw around the silky skin and causing goosebumps to appear.

Her hands flexed on the armrest.

Going lower, I let my teeth grab hold of the top of her black lace thong. I pulled at it, letting the fabric slide between her pussy lips and rub her clit.

She whimpered and ground against the material.

I released her underwear and then immediately grabbed it with my hands, snapping the sides.

"Baz. Those were expensive." The incredulous look on her face had me grinning.

I'd never been the type to smile this much while trying to seduce any woman but then again, none of them were Eloisa Benz…Weber.

"I can afford to buy you more."

"I don't need you to buy me anything. I can buy it myself."

I grabbed hold of her thighs, tugged her forward, and perched her knees against my shoulders.

I looked down at her pants-bound feet and splayed thighs, exposing her slick swollen pussy and immediately felt a shot of precum leak from my cock. This woman was a goddess without trying.

"Duly noted."

Lowering my face, I blew on her damp slit a second before I descended.

"Oh God," Isa cried out as her hold on the chair tightened.

I fucked my tongue into her tight cunt, pumping, rolling, and licking.

She tasted like heaven, something I could never get enough of.

One of her hands shifted to my head and I growled, "Put that hand back."

"Fuck. Sorry," she said while complying.

Her mewled cries grew louder as her pussy quickened and her hips rose to meet the demands of my mouth.

Pushing my hands under her shirt, I pulled the cups of her bra to the side and pinched her nipples until she moaned and her pussy juices flooded my mouth.

"Baz. Harder."

My woman liked the edge of pain.

I squeezed harder, releasing her tight buds a second before I knew it was too much, while continuing to tease her clit.

My cock was so hard it was a wonder I hadn't torn through my pants.

The first thing I planned to do the minute she arrived at our penthouse was bend her over the back of the nearest couch and fuck her hard.

"Baz. Oh God, Baz. I need to come. Make me come."

I stared up at her beautiful face, flushed with need. Lowering one hand to her soaked slit, I pushed a finger into her quivering pussy and curled it up until I grazed the sensitive bundle of nerves deep in her.

With one last lick to her delicious cunt, she detonated, thrashing her head side to side and digging her nails into the arms of her chair.

Watching her come apart was like nothing I'd ever experienced before. I would never get tired of seeing the ecstasy on her face or the way she responded to me.

She was mine and I'd protect her until my dying breath.

"Wow," Isa exclaimed after she'd finally come down from her orgasm.

I pushed her knees together and then adjusted her body back onto the chair.

"I'm glad you enjoyed that."

She leaned forward, gripping my shirt and pulling me toward her. Her kiss was hot and hard, and my straining dick ached to be inside her.

Her fingers roamed along the buttons of my shirt and then to the fastening of my pants. Just as she was about to pop the button, I stayed her hand.

"Don't you want me to return the favor?"

My cock screamed yes but I knew I couldn't push it.

"I'm positive one of our people is going to interrupt us at any moment."

As if on cue, a knock sounded on the door. "Boss. There's someone here to see you."

Isa's relaxed and sensual demeanor disappeared. "Um. Give me ten minutes. I'll be right out."

She stood, pulling her jeans up with her. I steadied her as she lost balance.

"Boss, it's Bri Amici. She needs to see you immediately."

I froze. What the hell was Isa doing with a Solon agent? An agent who'd been a handler on my last assignment, specifically for Ana Kipos.

"Tell her to wait. She's always got something urgent and likes to rush people."

Isa hurried into the bathroom adjacent to her office. I rose, inhaling deep to keep calm as I thought about all the things she could be doing for Solon. If she was an agent, I'd have heard about it, especially if she was assigned to any of the European divisions. The fact this bit of information had been kept from me only meant it had been scrubbed from the search I'd requested from Interpol.

Fuck, someone in Interpol had kept this from me.

I moved to the bathroom door and leaned against the wall outside it, waiting for Isa to emerge.

The second she did, I asked, "Why are you meeting with a Solon agent?"

Her eyes grew big. "How do you know about Bri?"

"You answer my question and I'll answer yours."

"She hired me to appraise some items she collected."

Her answer was plausible, but nothing was that simple when Solon was involved. They liked to recruit people with connections and ties to all walks of life and usually people with backgrounds of affluence. They also had no qualms about using tactics that broke the law to achieve their goals.

"And?"

She glared at me. "An answer for an answer."

I knew I had to give a little. "I've helped Bri with a few assignments."

"What kinds of assignments?" Worry flashed across her face, telling me she knew that Bri specialized in the division involved in handling sex-trafficking cases.

"Are you thinking I can't take care of myself, Isa?"

"No. She…she has a habit of working on the most dangerous of projects."

I picked up her hand and brought it to my face, kissing her fingertips. "I need you to remember I'm only Baz with you. In the outside world, I'm Sebastian Weber, notorious businessman and now head of one of the most dangerous organizations in Europe. My reputation isn't fabricated."

An impatient knock rapped on the door.

"*Bella*, open the door. I wait for no one. You can fuck on your own time," a voice called in Italian-accented German.

Isa groaned. "She has the spoiled Italian socialite thing down pat. No one would suspect she could kill a man in two moves."

"I heard that."

"We aren't done with this discussion." I stared into Isa's blue eyes.

"I wouldn't expect anything else." Isa moved to the door, unlocked it, and opened to a beautiful woman with a fur coat around her shoulders, a designer outfit hot off the runway, and a handbag worth a few hundred thousand Euros.

"Hello, *Herr* Weber." Her accent switched to one only a native German speaker could have pulled off.

There was mischief in her gaze that said she knew Isa was mine and what we were doing.

Which only meant she was here to cause trouble.

"*Signorina* Amici," I said with a perfect Italian inflection.

She scanned me from head to toe, lingering on my still half-hard cock a fraction too long before meeting my eyes. "Marriage looks good on you."

"You should try it. I know your intended would appreciate an official date."

The sneer that touched her lips nearly had me laughing. She'd been promised to one of the sons of her father's blue-blood friends. Someone I considered a friend and who happened to be in the same line of work I was in. Interpol and head of an organized family. Though his business revolved around financing the projects of other families.

I'd learned on one of my first joint operations with Solon that Bri had a low opinion of arranged marriages and never planned to follow through with hers. She'd created a very public spoiled-brat image to give reason for her never-ending engagement. Too bad for her, her fiancé was about to call her bluff.

"I'll let Isa tell me if it's worth the trouble and then perhaps entertain the idea." Her attention turned to Isa. "This is what you turned down my proposal for. *Bella*, I never expected you to go soft for a big dick."

Isa's face went deep red.

"On that note, I'll leave you ladies to finish business." I walked over to Isa, cupped the back of her head, and drew her in for a kiss. "We'll discuss your secret activities when you get home."

Before she could respond, I strode out the door.

CHAPTER THIRTEEN

Isa

"How do you know Ba…Sebastian? And why would you say the big-dick part in front of him?"

"Because the activities you didn't want me to see and made me wait for hadn't cooled in his blood."

Dear God, Bri had been checking out Baz's package. If I didn't know she was half in love with her unwanted fiancé, I'd have punched her.

That was probably not a good idea, since she was a spy and all that and could kill me without breaking a sweat. The pampered princess was a lethal weapon who'd taught me most of my moves.

"And the first part of my question?" I couldn't hide my annoyance.

A knowing smile touched Bri's lips. "My higher-ups

have kept an eye on him for years. He is… How do you say it?" She tapped her lips. "A person of interest."

That was a crock of bull.

There was something between Baz and Bri that rubbed me the wrong way. It was as if she knew more about my husband than I did.

Hell, she probably did.

The man I'd met over the last few months for coffee dates was a lie. One couldn't run an organized family like Sebastian's or be the son of an asshole like Jonas Weber and be the Baz I'd fallen for.

I guess time would reveal the truth.

The one thing I was sure of was that my husband could make me come over and over again. At least, we were sexually compatible.

"Could you be any vaguer?"

"Of course, I could."

"I really hate you sometimes. No wonder Ana quit on you."

"Ana quit because the reason for her leaving to join my circus came back for her and impregnated her. Pregnancy and the agency aren't a good combination."

She studied me and sighed. "You're going to be next. Deny he fucks you every chance he gets."

"We've been married less than a day."

"I know a woman who's tasted the goods before the purchase. Did you try to kill him when you found out he was pretending to be an ordinary businessman?"

I narrowed my gaze and smacked my desk. "You were

having me watched?" I threw my hands in the air. "You could have saved me the humiliation of finding out after the fact. Dammit, Bri, you're supposed to be on my side."

Bri shrugged. "I like both of you. And you weren't in danger. Weber protects his own. Besides, it was quite entertaining to see the unguarded side of both of you."

"Baz and I are not a fucking soap opera for your entertainment."

"Baz?"

I clenched my teeth. "If I didn't like you so much, I'd have quit helping you years ago."

"You love me, *bella*. Admit it. Especially since I bring you treats from your favorite bakery in Milano."

She pulled out a box from her handbag and handed it to me. Who the fuck keeps baked goods in a bag worth more than people's homes?

Briana Amici, of course.

I took the box and opened the lid, inhaling the sweet scent of *bomboloni*, an Italian version of doughnut holes, and cream-filled cannolis. Pulling one of the doughnuts out, I quickly hid the box in one of my desk drawers and then took a big bite of the doughy piece of heaven.

My staff always seemed to find their way to my office after one of Bri's visits and then would sucker me into sharing my stash of treats.

"Why are you here, Bri? Other than to annoy the crap out of me."

She walked over to my door, shut it, and then strolled to the seat across from my desk before sitting down.

"There's a hit out on Sebastian."

I stopped chewing and set my treat on a napkin. "Say that again."

"You heard me."

"How do you know this?"

"Some of our tech sleuths heard chatter on the web."

By "web," she meant the dark web. The part of the Internet ninety-nine percent of the world never accessed but where the dirtiest, darkest, and most dangerous deals occurred, from arms deals and assassination plots to the bartering of humans.

"Why are you telling me and not him?"

"Because our association isn't public knowledge." She paused, and then continued. "And he wouldn't believe me. Your husband is so used to having a target on his head, he doesn't take any new threat seriously. He's all business except when it comes to you. He deviated from the norm. He softened for you. He'll listen to you."

I found it hard to believe.

As if seeing my doubt, she said, "I've known him for the last five years. He handles his business efficiently and has a single-minded focus toward his goals. You are the one person he has put everything on hold for. He spent time with you, he got to know you, he showed you a side of him no one, I mean *no one*, has ever seen."

The way she described Sebastian reminded me of Papa. The people he softened with were Mama and me.

"What do you expect me to do? We've been married less than a day."

"I need you to get him out of town."

"I can't leave, I have multiple fucking businesses to run."

"Your able-bodied staff is more than capable of handling them until we can determine who the threat is on his life."

"Why is this so important to you?"

"I owe him, and I always pay my debts."

"What did he do for you?"

"That is a need to know." She stood, pulling out a folder from her bag and tossing it on my desk. "Look over these pieces and give me a price for appraisal."

"I already told you I can't do it."

"You know you want to. You like the game of finding the fakes from the real thing."

She was right, but I wasn't going to admit it. I wasn't secret-agent material, but it was a hell of a lot of fun to discover a master forger when no other person around had caught on.

"You're so bossy."

"That's the only way to be, *bella*. Now get your man out of town."

"You seem to think higher of my abilities than I do. And what excuse could I possibly give him?"

"Pretend you want to go on a honeymoon. You're a princess, sometimes you need to act like one."

I sobered as the gravity of why Bri wanted me to leave with Sebastian hit me. "I won't lie to him. Lies are what caused the mess between us."

"I swear, you're so annoying with your 'tell the truth'

ideals. Sometimes a little white lie keeps danger from invading one's world."

"Some people are trained to lie. I'm not. I suck at it."

"That you do. Remember that time I told you to tell the art dealer his statue was a fake when it wasn't? You nearly stuttered your way into a heart attack."

I pinched my lips together. It was my one-and-only time working face-to-face with a target.

"I prefer to focus on my skills as a markswoman in stopping said dealer from running away with his stolen goods."

"You shot the tires out of his car, from the roof of the building. I hardly think that was a good use of the hours I spent teaching you to handle a long-range rifle. If you're going to shoot, shoot the perp, not the car."

"You may have taught me to shoot, but Ana's the one who honed my skills."

"Well, she quit so now you're stuck with me."

"Whatever. I'm not going to lie to him."

"I'm not telling you to lie. Besides, he's like a human lie detector."

"I really hate you sometimes."

"It's okay. I love you all the time."

S ebastian

. . .

"What's the emergency?" I said to Lucas as I returned to Jonas's townhouse.

The last thing I wanted to do was come back to this godforsaken place. I had hours of calls to make to all of my family's allies, informing them of the change in power.

But the cryptic text Lucas sent, saying, *Urgent, get your ass back to the house and put a man on your bride*, had me driving back in an hour and putting everything else on hold.

Assigning someone to protect Isa wasn't a problem. I'd had a man on her since the moment I learned I was engaged to her. The combination of my people with her personal detail would keep her as protected as possible without keeping her under lock and key.

Instead of answering my question, Lucas said, "If you don't kill him after this, I will. It's in his bedroom."

The thought of going into the room where the old man had spent the years since Mama's death with his near-underaged girls made me want to hurl. It hadn't even been a month after Mama's funeral when one of his women had paraded through the house as if she were queen of the manor.

She'd learned she was disposable a week later when she was replaced by another beauty with a killer body and no ambition but to land a man by spreading her legs.

We made our way into the musty, over-decorated house. We entered the bedroom to find a group of soldiers emptying drawers and one digging through a safe that looked freshly installed.

"Bring them here," Lucas said to Kurt, who seemed to have a slight edge of worry on his face.

"Sir, you need to see this." Kurt handed me a file folder and then positioned an open laptop in my direction.

Inside the folder were more pictures of Isa, but these were shots designed to be part of an investigative profile, similar to the one I'd had made on her. But instead of details on her whereabouts, it had information on her sexual history and physical measurements.

The coldness I'd felt when I'd seen the pictures from earlier in the morning returned.

As I flipped to the last of the documents in the folder, I found a transcript of a phone conversation Jonas had had a little over six months ago with Carson Malkovich, a known member of a Russian family trying to create a stronghold in Germany. A family who specialized in the very thing I'd spent my last assignment stopping. The sale of humans.

They discussed past transactions and payments, but it was the end of the conversation that had me ready to find the bastard, beat him until he begged for death, and then leave him to freeze on the banks of the river.

Jonas: *Payment of forty million Euros upon completion of job. She's a prime piece of ass to populate your next generation.*

Malkovich: *I don't want a washed-up woman. I want her in breeding condition.*

Jonas: *The boy will use her but he won't hurt her—she's too much like his whore mother.*

Malkovich: *What guarantees do I have that this won't blow up in our faces?*

Jonas: *I know my organization and my men. Their loyalty will always be to me. You'll have to trust me.*

Malkovich: *I trust no one.*

Jonas: *You still owe me for what happened to my Hannah.*

Malkovich: *I owe you nothing. My men did what you arranged. It was your responsibility to have your daughter with you.*

Jonas: *You want the girl or not?*

Malkovich: *Forty million and the girl. Immediately upon delivery.*

Jonas: *Excellent. Now to get the boy.*

The rage coursing through my body took all my effort not to let loose. My mind was swimming. All these years of not knowing, of wondering, of searching.

I clenched my fists. Jonas had been responsible for Mama and Hannah's deaths. He'd destroyed an amazing woman and a sweet little girl.

And now he was going to sell my wife to a man who not only had killed my mother and sister but every one of his women after torturing them first.

The room seemed to still as if everyone was waiting for my reaction. I'd spent too many years schooling my responses to give anything away.

Taking a deep breath, I turned to Kurt and took the laptop he held. That was when I noticed the only soldiers in the room were those who'd been with me since I was a teenager. None of the ones from earlier in the morning were here.

If Lucas had removed everyone who was under Jonas, he had to have suspicions about loyalty, especially after what Jonas had said in the transcript.

I glanced at Lucas, who gestured with his chin to the computer. "Take a look at what we found on the surveillance footage from the family airstrip an hour after Jonas left here."

My gaze shifted to the screen. There was a picture of Jonas boarding a plane.

"That's not one of our jets." I studied the luxury aircraft.

"It's Malkovich's."

"Who cleared it to land? Ben?"

Ben was one of my men—he would never betray me.

Lucas's gaze grew harder than before. "No. Andre found his body half an hour ago. Ben was shot and then his throat was slit."

That was the signature move for Malkovich's people.

Fuck. Ben had a wife and kids. He'd moved to the airfield believing it was a safer position than being my security detail.

Jonas had planned all of this. He'd sacrificed a good man.

"Why the fuck didn't we get a warning the airstrip was in use?"

"Because Jonas ensured we wouldn't." Kurt pointed to the screen.

Circled in bold red were the faces of Dax and Samuel Walter. They stood at the base of the stairs of the plane Jonas boarded, and from their demeanor, they weren't just with Jonas, they were with Malkovich.

How long had they played both sides?

The sense of betrayal was a punch to the gut. They were two high-ranking lieutenants in the organization, who'd been around since *Opa* had run the family. I'd trusted them. They'd helped me get my head on straight after my mother and sister's murders. They'd played at loyalty to the family above all things.

Liars. They sacrificed the life of one of our men and put my wife in mortal danger.

Those bastards were going to learn the cost of siding with anyone other than the family.

"Did they come back after dropping Jonas off?" I asked, to no one in particular. This time I couldn't hide the rage boiling in me.

Lucas answered, "Yes. They're in the basement. I have them searching the files for information on Jonas's safe houses."

"I'm sure they liked that task."

Dax and Samuel were at the top of the food chain under Jonas, but with me they wouldn't have that place. They'd have to prove they were worthy of their positions.

That was a moot point now.

"They haven't quite grasped I'm your second and if I tell them to scrub toilets, they need to shut their mouths and do it."

"Kurt, you're in charge. Secure the room. I believe it's time to have a chat with the Walter brothers."

Not bothering to see if my instructions were followed, I turned and made my way to the basement.

As I approached, I heard Dax say, "They're beauties. Too bad you don't have a taste for them."

"Shut the fuck up. If anyone hears you, Weber won't think twice about ending us," Samuel responded.

"The boy needs us. We know all of his father's secrets. How else is he going to locate him?" The amusement in Dax's tone said he had no qualms about double-crossing me.

I slowly stepped into the room, my men staying quiet behind me. Neither Dax nor Samuel noticed my entrance.

"You're too cocky. You saw the way he watched his woman. This isn't going to be as cut and dry as everyone believes." Samuel opened another box. "Why the fuck does one man need all this useless shit?"

"That's not our business. Boss wanted it kept. All you have to do is follow the plan."

It was time to make my presence known. "Mind sharing this plan? Especially since I'm your boss."

Both men froze.

I walked up to them. "I gave an order."

The way their eyes shifted back and forth as if they were looking for an escape had me almost hoping they'd try something. The men were big, but untrained from years of giving orders.

"Not sure what plan you're talking about." Dax rose

from his perch over a box and came toward me. "We're just following Flynn's directive." There was a sneer in his words that had me holding back the urge to backhand him.

I held out a hand, and immediately, Lucas placed the switchblade *Opa* had given me before his death into it, the very one he'd used when disciplining his soldiers.

At the sound of the knife opening, Dax made a run for the window, the only way out. Before he could make it a few steps, I grabbed him by the hair, threw him to the ground, and stabbed the knife into the hand he was about to use to leverage himself up.

"What's gotten into you, boy?" Dax roared.

Pressing a foot to his throat, I leaned over him, pulling my blade free, and almost immediately Dax kicked up, trying to knock me back, but I shifted and stuck him with the blade in the ribs.

"Stop struggling or I'll make sure with one twist of my wrist, you'll breathe out of a tube for your short foreseeable future."

Blood seeped from Dax's hand and from the wound in his side where my knife sat.

"Listen, dammit!" Samuel shouted. "The money's not worth your life."

Dax's eyes bulged as I pressed the hilt of the knife deeper, but he didn't move.

"Now I want you to tell us everything. You leave anything out, you're dead. You hedge, you're dead. You lie to me, you're dead. And you," I said to Samuel, who remained near the boxes he'd been opening. "If he leaves anything out, or prevents me from protecting my bride, you will suffer a slow, torturous death. Make sure no detail is missing."

Pulling out the knife, I wiped it on Dax's shirt, handed it to Lucas, and rose.

"You know the drill. Extract every last detail from them and make it painful."

"I'll take care of it."

"Contact Benz and set up a meeting." I knew I wouldn't have to say more than that. Lucas would handle everything.

Now all I had to do was convince my wife to leave the country without letting her know my father had planned to sell her in order to take back his empire.

CHAPTER FOURTEEN

Sebastian

I arrived at my penthouse a little before six in the evening to find bags in the foyer. Some were mine and others were the ones Isa had delivered the morning of our wedding.

Why the fuck would Isa have packed for me? Where was she planning for us to go?

Then I stopped. Had someone called and told her I was taking her away? That still didn't make sense. No one would overstep, especially not Lucas and especially not after word got out that Dax and Samuel were permanently removed from the Weber infrastructure.

"Isa."

There was no response. I made my way toward our bedroom. *Our bedroom.* That's what it was. And I'd be dammed if it wasn't going to stay ours. If Jonas thought he could double-cross me, take the money *Opa* allotted for him, and still remain king, then he had another think coming.

As of five minutes after I saw the pictures of him boarding the plane, I'd sent word to every family, ally or not, that any aid or harbor rendered to Jonas Weber meant a declaration of war.

I'd lost my mother and sister to Jonas's schemes. I was not going to lose Isa.

Hell, to protect her, I'd done the one thing no one would ever expect me to do. I'd gone to Russo Benz.

The man hated me on principle. Knowing I had nothing to do with the deal *Opa* made with his father didn't change his anger at losing control of the empire he'd built. I had a great deal of respect for the man—he'd taken the small organization his father had left him and created something ten times bigger.

He was a hard, ruthless man, but there was no doubt in my mind that he loved his daughter and would do everything possible to keep her safe.

When I told him what Jonas was planning, he had nearly lost his mind with the drive to take out Jonas. But he knew the rules and he couldn't move on Jonas without consequences to the rest of us. Isa now belonged to me. He'd agreed to use his resources to keep an eye on Jonas through his Russian connections as well as my territory while I was away with Isa.

It was a show of trust I'd given Benz that no boss with

my sized organization would ever have given. This gesture had shifted something between us, and I knew I had an ally.

As I entered the bedroom, the last words Benz had said before I'd left his house lingered in my head.

There are three things you need to do, and I will pledge my loyalty to you. Take care of my little girl, treat her right, and make her happy. Whatever you did to hurt her, fix it. I know my girl knew you before yesterday. I saw it in her eyes when the chapel doors opened. I'm not going to ask how. I'm not going to ask when it started. All I am saying is bring her back to the Isa I knew.

Isa was his heart. It wouldn't matter to him that she still hadn't forgiven him or his wife for forcing the marriage. She was his baby, his only child.

I had a new respect for him. He didn't view having a daughter as a liability. As far as anyone knew, Russo never kept a mistress to have other children with. This was a standard practice among organized families. For a mobster, he'd taken his marriage vows as a sacred bond. Something I had no problems doing as well.

"Isa?" I called again, right before the sound of rushing water hit my ears.

Moving to the bathroom, I pushed open the door and was hit by a billow of steam. The silhouette of Isa's curvy body through the frosted glass of the shower enclosure was like a peepshow. One only I'd ever enjoy.

There was a possessiveness when I saw her. I'd felt it that first night in the club. I'd felt it more and more as we'd met for our coffee dates. And now that we were married, I felt it to the depths of my dark soul.

My cock hardened as I watched her pour liquid onto her sponge and lather her body. Her movements weren't meant to be seductive, but my body didn't care. I shouldn't want someone like this. I'd fucked her all night.

No, she'd fucked me all night. I'd let her hold the reins —well, for the most part—so she could purge her rage at me. Now we were in new territory, one we'd both have to learn to navigate.

She did things the way she wanted. I knew she wasn't stupid—as Benz's beloved daughter she couldn't be. But as my wife, it was a whole new level. This would have to change. She wouldn't be able to go anywhere without proper protection. She had her own protection, but I trusted her life to no one but my own men.

Once I was naked, I stroked my cock and moved to the shower. She still had no idea I was in the bathroom, watching her.

She jumped as I opened the door, dropping her sponge and turning to face me, her back against the shower wall.

The multiple showerheads beating against her skin made her look like a literal wet dream. She was perfect, the right curves in the right places, a mouth meant for wrapping around my cock, and eyes so blue, it felt like she could see into the depths of my soul.

She studied me, her gaze lingering on my cock, watching me pump the hard length from root to tip. She licked her lips, and I almost groaned. He nipples grew hard and her skin flushed, not from the heat of the water but her growing arousal.

I released my grip, letting my dick smack against my stomach, and closed the stall door without taking my focus away from her.

She lifted a hand to keep me back. "I need to talk to you. It's important."

"Does it have to do with the bags at the front door?" I moved closer until her palm pressed to my chest.

"Yes. We have to get out of town. Bri said you're in danger."

What the hell had Bri told her after I'd left them alone?

Bri was always hearing one thing or another planned against the Weber heir. She should know as well as I did that my commanders in Interpol would have warned me.

I was going to have to warn Bri against panicking my wife. Though it seemed pushing Isa's need to protect me had worked in my favor. I wouldn't have to convince her to leave, and I wouldn't have to tell her why I wanted to take her away.

Idiot. A lie of omission is still a lie. Didn't you learn the first time?

"It's part of being a Weber, Isa. You should know that same thing goes for your father."

"Bri said the threat is credible. It came from underground chatter."

I redirected her hand until it gripped my cock, pumping up and down.

"You're not listening."

She released me, ready to shift around me, but I caught her at the waist and pressed my aroused body to the front of her water-soaked one.

"My life is all about threats. You're the one who I need to worry about. Now if someone threatened you, then I'd take drastic precautions." I slid my engorged cock between her legs and her swollen pussy lips, making sure to nudge her pussy.

"I won't let you seduce me into forgetting about my concerns." Her voice was raspy now, her desire winning out.

"What do you suggest I do?"

"I want to leave town." Her pussy grew slicker as I teased her with my cock. "Bri…Bri said she'll contact you with details."

Oh, I was going to contact Bri, all right, but right now I was going to fuck my wife.

"If I agree to go out of town will you calm down?"

"Not just out of town. We have to get out of Europe altogether."

I should feel bad that she was saying the exact thing I'd been going to tell her. But I wouldn't look a gift horse in the mouth.

"Fine. Though I have one question for you."

I skimmed my hand up the side of her body.

"What?"

I cupped her throat and felt her pulse jump as her cobalt eyes dilated. "Does your worry about me mean you care?"

She narrowed her gaze. "You know I do."

"Do I? If I recall, last night you told me you hated me." I leaned in, rubbing my stubble against her jaw.

A moan escaped her lips, and she tilted her neck to give me better access as her palms worked their way up my chest and around my neck. I licked the beads of water spraying on her skin. Her nipples pebbled harder.

"I don't hate you. I should, but I don't."

I pulled her face to look at me. "Then what do you feel?"

"What do you feel for me?" she countered.

I knew she felt exactly what I felt, something neither of us wanted to give words to. Something that would make her my greatest weakness.

Who the fuck was I kidding? She *was* my greatest weakness and the reason Jonas had used her as leverage against me.

Instead of answering, I lifted her up by the thighs, spread her legs, positioned my cock, and thrust home.

"Baz." She threw her head back and clutched my hair and my shoulder.

I pumped in and out of her in a hard, ruthless tempo, feeling the anger of what I'd discovered returning.

"Tell me, Isa."

"No."

I pushed in all the way and rolled my hips, pressing the base of my cock along her sensitive clit. Just as I felt her pussy walls quiver and clench, I pulled out and stilled again, with the head poised just in her entrance.

"Don't stop. Dammit. I'm almost there." She smacked at my back and tried to use her legs to force me forward.

"Not until you give me the words."

"You're not being fair." She shook her head. "Why do you want so much from me when you don't give me anything?"

Even through the spray of the shower, I could see her tears.

Threading my fingers into her hair, I stared into her eyes.

"You're mine, Isa."

"What does that mean?"

I shook the water dripping onto my face and dropped my forehead to hers, still holding her gaze.

The feelings I had for her were too intense to put into words, but I knew I had to try. The last few months had meant more to me than any other time in my life.

"It means I'm never letting you go."

Thrust.

"It means I'll kill anyone who tries to take you from me."

Thrust.

"It means you're my weakness. A man like me can't afford to have weaknesses."

Thrust.

"I'll destroy the world to protect you."

Her breath was ragged as I worked her cunt and she took in my words.

"I don't want you to destroy the world. I just need you."

I stopped moving again.

"What does that mean, Isa?"

I saw the hesitation before she said, "It means…I love you, Baz. I should hate you for lying to me, for everything that was forced on me, but I don't. I fell in love with you. Why did you make me love you?"

My heart nearly exploded hearing her words. She loved me. I finally had someone who was mine. Truly mine.

"Because you were born to be mine." My voice was gruff but I didn't care.

I covered my lips over hers and picked up the pace of my pistoning cock.

We spoke no more words as the need to come overtook us. Kissing, tasting, fucking.

Her nails scored my skin and she met each of my thrusts with the demands of her body.

"Oh God, oh God. Baz. I'm coming. I'm coming."

"Come, baby, come," I growled through clenched teeth.

She spasmed and then clamped down around my cock so hard, I saw stars.

My body erupted along with her, shooting deep inside her.

I knew we should be using protection. We weren't ready for the next steps of life. But the thought of her round with my child brought out a primitive need to permanently tie her to me.

"Christ. You fucking feel incredible." My brain completely stopped except for the need to work out every drop of the cum in my body.

When I could move again, I realized I hadn't given her the words she'd given me. I wasn't sure I'd ever be able to. I'd just have to show her by keeping her safe. I would die to keep her safe. Hopefully it wouldn't come to that.

Isa

"Where are we going?" I asked Sebastian for the tenth time since we left on one of his private jets a little over an hour ago.

"Somewhere unexpected."

I pursed my lips and glared at him as he scanned papers at the desk across from where I sat.

"That doesn't tell me anything."

A slight curve to his mouth told me he was being vague on purpose.

I growled and pulled out the book Lilly had tucked into my bag when I'd stopped by our office to tell her we were going out of town for a few days.

Instead of grumbling about the appraisal of Bri's art collection that Lilly would have to do on her own, she'd all but jumped for joy. She assumed we were jetting off to a honeymoon destination and I hadn't corrected her notion.

Lilly was a hopeless romantic and needed someone who understood her big heart. Hopefully Kane saw this and gave her what she needed instead of blowing hot and cold with her. I didn't know much about Kane outside of the fact he ran Sebastian's club. I'd have to ask Sebastian about him.

Later. Once I knew where we were going. Once my annoying husband threw me a bone.

"Stop glaring at me. It's okay not to have control sometimes. I'm not going to take you anywhere you won't enjoy."

"Says the man with all the control. I'm surprised you let me fuck your brains out on our wedding night."

He lifted his dark gaze. "What makes you think I had no control in that situation? The one thing you aren't is a top, even if you are in fact on top."

My mind went to the way he'd held me as I rode him, the way he'd guided my movements, the way he'd made me come.

Fuck. He was right.

My cheeks heated.

"I don't like you having all the power in our relationship. It feels unbalanced."

Sebastian pushed back from his seat, not saying a word, and came toward me. When he was upon me, he crouched down, setting a hand on my thigh. His hold was possessive.

"Power and control are two different things." His fingers glided along my skin, brushing the hem of my dress. "Control is having the ability to focus on the needs and wants of your woman and giving it to her before taking your own pleasure."

Every nerve in my body fired to life as his touch moved higher.

"Power is the ability to drive a man to put aside everything he's ever focused on for his wife." His thumb skimmed the damp gusset of my underwear. "From the beginning, you've had all the power. I was at your mercy. I was ready to beg for just a sliver of your time, for the slightest taste of you. I spent months meeting you for coffee, knowing I'd rather have been buried deep in your cunt. You made me want things I didn't even know I wanted. If that isn't power, I don't know what is."

His fingers slid past my thong and plunged deep into my pussy, scissoring out. My body arched toward him as my head fell back against the cushions of the seat. The book in my lap fell to the floor with a thud.

"Baz." I closed my eyes, lost in the pleasure of his wicked hand.

"You're the only person who could get me on a plane in the middle of a takeover, during a time I had to assert my authority in my territory."

He thrust in and out, my arousal flooding his hand. "You hold all the power, Isa."

My vaginal muscles quickened and then clenched, my orgasm right upon me.

"But I control your pleasure and you don't come unless I let you." He abruptly withdrew, leaving me hanging.

"No. Baz. What are you doing?"

He grinned, bringing his fingers to his mouth and sucking my essence clean.

"You can't be serious. You're going to leave me hanging?"

"If we were in our cabin, then I might consider it, but we're here where anyone can see you." He leaned forward, taking my lips in a deep kiss.

I could taste myself, and it heightened the uncomfortable need deep inside me.

He straightened the skirt of my dress and picked up my book from the floor. Sebastian read the title, smirked, and then set it on my lap.

"I think this is great reading. Tell Lilly I said thank you." He rose and returned to his desk. Less than a second later, Denise, the flight attendant, entered the lounge with a tray of drinks and food.

"Be prepared," I muttered so only Sebastian could hear. "I'll get my revenge."

"I have no doubt that you'll try," he responded, not caring that Denise could hear everything we were saying. "Just remember I'm the one in control."

"Whatever. I can take care of it without your help," I said to Sebastian while smiling at Denise as she set my drink and a fruit-and-cheese plate in front of me.

"But you won't." He took his plate and drink, setting them on the desk.

I picked up a grape to pop into my mouth. "And why not?"

He turned his dark, almost black gaze toward me. The intensity of it had butterflies fluttering in my stomach. "Because the reward will be worth at least ten of them."

"Oh." I bit into the sweet fruit. "So, this is a type of game?"

"Something like that. I promise you won't regret it."

I knew I wasn't going to get what I wanted no matter how much my body needed relief.

"Fine. I'll wait."

Sebastian smirked. "You do that. In the meantime, why don't you read the book Lilly packed? I'm sure you'll find it fascinating reading material."

Was that humor I heard in his tone? I'd get my revenge, orgasms or not.

I grabbed the book Lilly had picked for me and nearly groaned. It was a copy of the *Kama Sutra* with pictures and detailed descriptions. I clenched my teeth.

Best friend or not, the woman was a menace.

Good thing I adored her.

CHAPTER FIFTEEN

Isa

"Isa. It's time to wake up."

"No," I moaned and rolled over. "I need a few more hours of sleep."

Sebastian chuckled. "You've slept for seven hours. It's time to get ready."

That's when I realized I was lying on a bed under luxurious covers that felt like the softest and highest thread-count cotton available against my skin.

My eyes snapped open. Sebastian leaned over me. He was bare-chested and his jaw was shadowed by a dark growth of beard, giving him a rakish look. His hair was wet, telling me he'd showered.

I peeked over his shoulder and took in the opulent room. It was decorated in soft neutral tones. So this was the private cabin. I'd flown on private jets before but none with a bedroom or shower. Then again, I'd only flown around Europe, where everything was within a few hours' flight, and one trip to see Ana in Las Vegas. But that had been on a commercial flight under an assumed name with a passport Ana had arranged for me.

"How did I get in here? The last thing I remember was watching one of the *Ocean's* movies."

I vaguely remembered curling into him when the plane hit some turbulence and then falling back asleep. I guessed it wasn't turbulence—it was Sebastian bringing me in here.

He shook his head. "You are one hard sleeper. You barely stirred when I undressed you and put you to bed."

At that moment, the sheets covering me slipped, revealing my naked body.

"Naked? Really?"

He lifted a brow. "I sleep naked. Therefore, you sleep naked."

His gaze shifted to my breasts, and my nipples immediately pebbled.

"Did you give me an orgasm while you were at it?" I frowned at him. "I think I would have woken up if it was ten."

"Still not over it, are you?"

"You're not the one with a case of lady blue balls."

He picked up my hand and set it over his erection, the one I hadn't noticed until now.

"You've had me in this state since I met you at the club.

It doesn't matter how many times I come deep in your cunt. It'll never be enough."

Instead of climbing off the bed, I straddled his lap, letting the lips of my sex cradle his cock. Just like I had during our wedding night.

"We're not having sex, no matter how tempting you are," Sebastian said even as his hands cupped my ass and rubbed my pussy against his cock, coating it in my arousal.

I kissed his neck, inhaling his intoxicating scent, and then nipped his skin with my teeth.

"I don't want to have sex." I pushed him onto his back. "Well, not the way you're thinking."

He relaxed back onto the bed, tucking his arms behind his head.

"Be my guest. If you'd rather I come in your mouth than your pussy, who am I to argue?"

Sliding off his body, I grabbed his thick cock, fisting the base. Damn, his dick was amazing. How he fucked me without tearing me in half was a wonder. But then again, he always had me so ready for him. The slight discomfort was well worth the pleasure.

"Are you going to stare at it or do something with it?"

Sebastian's question snapped me out of my thoughts and I squeezed him from root to tip and back down. Precum dripped from the slit on the bulbous head of his erection. My mouth watered for a taste of him, but instead of giving in to my desire, I licked the thick vein underneath.

"Fuck, that feels good."

I smiled and continued my exploration before I took him fully into my mouth, going so deep that he hit the back of my throat. Tears filled my eyes as I tried to hold off the gag reflex.

As if my discomfort aroused Sebastian more, his cock seemed to grow harder and thicker. With each downward movement, it became easier to take him. When his hand fisted in my hair to aid the movement of my mouth, I knew his orgasm was upon him.

I released him with a pop, pulling free of his hold, and walked to the bathroom, ignoring the sting of my lips and the wetness pooling between my thighs.

"Isa." Sebastian's growl was feral.

"As you said, I have the power. Especially when your dick is in my mouth. Now you get to suffer the same way I am."

S ebastian

"Don't be mad. You know you deserved it," Isa said as she took the steps leading onto the tarmac of McCarran International Airport in Las Vegas.

The temperature was cool and dry, a sharp contrast to the last time I'd been here. It was years ago, when I'd attended the University of Nevada, Las Vegas. It hadn't been my family's first choice of schools for me to attend, but then again, they had no idea I was a fresh recruit into the lower ranks of Interpol, and one of their best training facilities was in Nevada.

"I'm not mad."

"Sure, you aren't." Isa smirked, and for the first time since we landed, took in the mountains and buildings near us.

She turned to me, her eyes bright with excitement. "We're in Vegas."

Her joy cooled the irritation I'd felt since she'd walked away a few seconds before I blew my load down her throat.

"You need to remember. While we're here, we are Sebastian and Isa Kohl. Weber and Benz don't exist."

"As if I couldn't figure out that on my own. Kohl it is, but I need to tell you something."

"What?"

At that moment, a blacked-out Suburban pulled up and out stepped Hagen and Persephone Lykaios. Hagen with his tanned arms covered in ink and a natural scowl on his face towered over his beautiful, dark-haired, almost pixie-sized wife with her unique mixture of Greek and Indian heritage.

"Penny," Isa shouted and ran down the remainder of the stairs, her words to me forgotten.

"Isa."

The two women embraced and chattered, most of which I couldn't understand as they were switching between German and English without taking a breath. I hadn't realized Penny knew German.

Why was I surprised? She was a genius with a level of intelligence I'd only seen in one other person—her brother Adrian.

"We have to speak English here. You know the rules. Whatever country we're in, is the language we speak," Isa said as she took Penny's hands.

The way Isa spoke English was unlike anything I expected—it was eloquent with a hint of a British accent. It was probably because of all the years she'd spent in the United Kingdom studying.

Penny pursed her lips. "Come on. I haven't been to Germany since you opened your first club."

"Rules are rules." Isa shrugged her shoulders. "I'm not the one who made up the rules. You did."

"I'm your elder. You're supposed to let me have my way."

"Has that line ever worked on anyone?"

Penny shrugged. "It was worth a try. Come on, let's get you in the car."

The women walked hand in hand to the car.

Isa wasn't kidding when she'd said she was friends with Penny.

Hagen watched me with those eyes that had always seen too much. He'd spent most of his youth as a mob enforcer before going straight. Well, as straight as anyone in Vegas could go.

We clasped hands as I approached him, and let him pull me into a hug.

"It's been a long time. So you married our Eloisa Wolff."

Wolff?

Isa turned and glanced at me as she stepped into the car, humor in her gaze before returning her attention to whatever Penny was saying.

Well, that was what she'd been going to tell me. I should have figured that Isa would never let anyone know her family's connections unless it was absolutely necessary.

"Yes, I married her. She's a Kohl now."

Hagen smirked. "If that's the way we're going to play it, I'll go along."

Hagen had been one of the first to figure out neither Adrian nor I were normal college students. He'd kept our secrets, never asking who we actually worked for. Though Adrian had told him when he went to work for Hagen and his brothers, I had never revealed my ties.

Nevertheless, I was positive he knew of my connection to Interpol and my family.

"How's Adrian?" I was looking forward to seeing the man who'd been my best friend for the past ten years.

It had been a blow when he'd stepped down and severed all ties to me. But then again, he'd spent most of our friendship undercover as another man. He was CIA, and the only way to start over was to kill the life he'd lived, including all relationships. It was cleaner and safer that way.

"Keeping Ana from overdoing it. Pregnancy has made

her a bit impatient to finish projects before her due date and moody when we tell her to sit down. Adrian takes the brunt of her wrath."

The mention of Ana had me cringing inside. It was a risk bringing Isa here and having her find out I'd slept with one of her close friends, but it was a risk I was willing to take.

Being around the Lykaios and Kipos families would keep her safer than any other place I could think of. They took protecting their loved ones to a level like nothing I'd seen outside of organized families.

I'd sent word to Adrian that we needed to lay low, disappear in the world of Vegas. There were too many high-profile people here for anyone to notice two Germans.

"Is everything arranged?"

"Yes. Nothing will happen to her while you're here. Your men arrived and are in place."

Which meant no one would know they were around unless they wanted to be seen. They were a mixture of Weber soldiers and members of security agencies who took on jobs between assignments.

"I've set you up in the penthouse at Ida. It has a separate elevator system and entrance."

"I appreciate you accommodating us."

Hagen narrowed his gaze. "I know you helped save Ana when her assignment went south. You helped bring her home. That debt can never be repaid."

Well, I wasn't expecting that. I wasn't going to question

how he'd heard about the details of the assignment—that was information Adrian and Ana managed.

"It isn't a debt. Ana is Adrian's, and that's all that mattered."

"We'll agree to disagree." He turned. "Let's get your lady settled."

CHAPTER SIXTEEN

Isa

As we pulled up to the curved drive of the Ida Casino and Resort, I was struck by the sheer size of the place. It was like an elegant sculpture of towers and buildings designed to stand out against the light of Vegas without looking gaudy.

"It's pretty incredible, isn't it?" Penny asked, with a hint of pride in her voice. "You should see it from the main entrance. Then you'll get a real feel for the place."

The hotels and casinos of Monte Carlo and Saint Tropez were elegant and had an aura of old-world money that made you feel inadequate to enter, but this one drew you in and made you want to explore.

"I'll take her around the hotel once we settle in," Sebastian said, taking my hand as the door opened.

Attendants immediately approached us, pulling the bags from the back of the SUV and carting them inside the hotel.

"We will see you both for lunch tomorrow at my house," Penny said. "Don't keep her out too late, Sebastian."

"I make no promises." Sebastian stepped out first before helping me onto my feet.

I waved to Penny as the car drove away and tucked my arm into Sebastian's. He guided me into the residential lobby, and I couldn't help but gape at the extraordinary chandelier hanging from the ceiling. It was a striking mixture of clear and reddish-gold glass and nearly took up the entire space of the ceiling.

"Holy shit." I tilted my head back to get a better look.

"I thought you said you've been to Vegas before."

"I have, but under disguise and never as a guest at the hotel. I stayed at the tower apartment Ana had before she married Adrian. We tended to avoid any place the Lykaios brothers would catch sight of us."

"Then when did you meet them?"

"At Sunday brunch. It's a thing they do once a month. It was a lot of fun. I beat the brothers at poker when we played. I even beat Penny, and she's ruthless. Though I lost every time to Henna. The woman is a card shark."

Sebastian stared at me as if I'd grown two heads.

"What?"

"You played poker against the Lykaioses?"

"Why are you so surprised? They play cards after brunch when the younger kids are napping."

"And you beat them?"

"All of them but Henna."

"Who taught you to play?"

"Papa. He's a great strategist. He always said I had to think ahead and keep my cool. So that's what I did."

Sebastian tugged me toward him and kissed my head. "You're one insane woman."

"Well, yeah. I'm with you."

Before he could retort, a tall, golden-tanned man approached us wearing the hotel uniform. "Mr. and Mrs. Kohl. I'm Eduardo, the desk manager. Welcome to the Ida Residence. Your personal elevator is over this way. If you would follow me."

We stopped in an alcove housing a single elevator.

"Mr. Kipos programmed the code per your specific request for the elevator and penthouse. Please enjoy your stay."

Sebastian inclined his head in thanks and then set a hand on my lower back to guide me into the elevator. When the doors closed, I studied Sebastian's reflection in the mirrors lining the cab walls.

Damn, he was one hot man. Not just in looks, but in the way he carried himself. He had this dangerous aura that would make any woman want to get closer. It was probably what drew me to him in the first place. If only I could trust this thing between us to be more than one sided. He'd gotten me to confess my feelings, but he'd never said the words to me.

I needed the words. But then again, could I trust him if he said them?

"What?" he asked, giving me a curious look.

"I was admiring the man who belongs to me. You're beautiful."

His lips curved as he held my gaze. "You're the one who's beautiful. Those eyes that grow to a deeper shade of blue when you're aroused, the mouth that gives a man visions of lips wrapped around his cock, and a body meant for fucking."

He turned, grabbed hold of my waist, and backed me against the cab railing.

"Then there's your temper. The fire of it says the passion you unleash will be all consuming and uncontrollable."

"Baz," I whispered and lifted my face, giving in to the seduction of his words and the desire to kiss him.

Before our lips could touch, the elevator doors opened, breaking the trance we were under.

I stepped into the penthouse and gasped.

This was like nothing I'd seen before. The expanse of the place was unbelievable. The windows made up the outer walls of the space, giving views of every angle of Las Vegas and the desert surrounding it.

There was a balcony off the living room that resembled a spa retreat with flowers and plants all around, more than likely designed to give the senses a break from the hustle and bustle of the busy city below.

The kitchen was state of the art, and the furniture

throughout was modern and clean, following the look of the rest of the resort.

This was no ordinary rentable penthouse. This had to be the infamous penthouse Ana said had belonged to Hagen that she'd used before she moved into her house.

"Impressive, isn't it?" Sebastian came up to me, setting a hand on my back.

"That's an understatement." I looked up at Sebastian. "This could rival our place in Berlin."

"But our view is better."

He was right. Our penthouse overlooked the river and had a calming effect on the senses. Views of the Strip could overwhelm the senses, especially for someone who spent a lot of time working in solitude.

"Very true. I like the craziness of Las Vegas for the short term, but anything longer than a week or two at a time would be too much to handle."

"If you want a place in Vegas to visit for quick trips, I'm sure one of the Lykaioses has a property available."

"I'm good. Besides, if I were going to buy a place from any of the Lykaioses, it would be from Henna. The woman knows real estate."

Henna Anthony-Lykaios was Ana's half sister and wife to Zack Lykaios. She'd been Zack's rival when it came to property development. Then they fell in love and now they were on a mission to populate Nevada with their offspring. Rumor had it, Henna was pregnant with baby number six and it had barely been four months since she gave birth to her little girl.

"Duly noted. What would you like to do tonight?"

I wanted to say *have multiple orgasms*, since my body hadn't come down from our airplane escapades. Instead, I answered with, "You decide."

"How about we check out Hagen's club?"

I smiled. "That's a perfect idea."

"Holy shit. You're gorgeous."

I beamed at Sebastian's reaction as I stepped out into the living room of the penthouse an hour later.

He walked up to me, offering his hand. I slid my palm over his, feeling a tingle of energy sizzle between us.

"You don't look too bad yourself." I let my gaze trail up and down his body.

The correct word for the way he looked was hot. Fucking hot. With whipped cream and a cherry on top.

This man epitomized sex appeal. His fitted black textured shirt and dark denim jeans accentuated his honed body and height. He'd pushed up the sleeves of his shirt, revealing his tattooed arms.

My libido was on overdrive and I wanted him on me, in me, any way I could get him.

"How about we skip the club and get naked?"

"Horny, baby?"

I frowned. "You know very well I am. What are we waiting for? We just got married. We're supposed to fuck like rabbits."

"It's called delayed gratification."

"Delayed gratification, my ass." I stalked to the elevator, dragging Sebastian behind me. "Come on, let's burn off our frustrations."

Sebastian seemed unfazed and followed without a word.

The moment we entered Nyx, the world-famous nightclub, my annoyance with my husband and my hormones was gone.

The pictures I'd seen hadn't done the place justice. The straight lines and neutral interior of the property flowed into here but there was a more sensual vibe. Splashes of reddish-gold were everywhere from the light fixtures to the statues.

"Holy fuck. Those are real." I pointed to a set of Greek figurines positioned in a wall alcove above the dance floor. "Those have to be worth ten million apiece."

"I guess you aren't the only one who gets to claim they have original artwork in their clubs."

"It's not something I advertise. I just thought it fit, and I happened to own the pieces."

"Come, let's dance."

We made our way onto the dance floor, and immediately Sebastian pulled me against him.

"The last time we danced together, I had to let you go. Tonight, I go home with you."

"Too bad sex doesn't seem to be on the menu."

We rolled our hips and bodies to the rhythm of the music, completely in tune with each other.

He danced like a man who knew what he was doing. His moves were commanding yet sensual, almost seducing.

We stayed on the dance floor through three tracks, lost in the beat.

Sebastian's hands slid up the sides of my body and then one fisted the hair at the nape of my neck as the other settled on my back, drawing me flush against him.

"You're my every fantasy come to life."

He was aroused, and the hunger in his dark eyes had my breath unsteady and my sex growing slick with need.

He'd left me hanging all day and I was desperate for release.

"Baz, I want to go to bed."

"Are you sure?"

I rubbed my pelvis against his thick, hard cock. "Absolutely."

"Then let's go." He picked up my hand and kissed my fingers before linking his with mine and leading me out of the club.

CHAPTER SEVENTEEN

Sebastian

"Are you still mad at me?" I asked Isa as we drove to Adrian and Ana's estate where the Lykaios-Kipos clan were waiting for our arrival.

"I'm not as mad but you're not my favorite person right now. What you did was wrong on so many levels."

I almost laughed at the incredulous scowl Isa shot in my direction.

Our night hadn't ended the way she'd expected. Instead of tearing off her clothes and burying my cock deep in her as I wanted to, I'd helped her undress and tucked her into bed.

I knew she was shocked and completely pissed off, but she'd complied, no doubt plotting some sort of revenge like the one she'd implemented on the jet.

The fact she had fallen asleep within minutes of me turning off the light hadn't mattered, she'd still woken up in a piss-poor mood, barely saying two words to me all morning.

I knew I had to tread carefully, so I did the one thing I was positive would get her temper calmer. I'd taken her to a range, the very one where Adrian and I had met during training. The one run through joint agency cooperation under the guise of a private shooting club.

The second Isa realized where we were, her frown disappeared, replaced by an eager calmness that was both unsettling and intriguing.

For someone born to be a pampered princess, her fascination with guns confused the hell out of me. I wasn't sure what kind of introduction she'd received from Bri in firearms, but Isa was a fanatic. It was more about mastering a skill versus using her ability for a fight.

Her ability was something I'd read about, but seeing it in person was beyond impressive. Watching her focus as she hit the bullseye of every single target she shot at was eerily arousing. If I'd told her this bit of news, she'd probably say I deserved it for torturing her.

If she wasn't my wife and I'd met her a few years earlier, I'd have recruited her for the agency.

That was when I'd realized she already worked for one in particular, Solon. Now that I thought about it, I'd heard about an antiquities expert based out of Germany the Berlin office of Interpol would call in on various cases.

It had to be Isa. We were definitely going to have a long conversation about her "clients."

Before I could even broach the subject, I was going to have to tell Isa the truth about Interpol and most of all about what had happened with Ana and Adrian on our last assignment.

Pushing back the doom I knew was going to come sooner rather than later, I focused on the game I was playing with Isa.

"I promise, the wait will be worth it."

She mumbled something under her breath as we pulled up to the front of a large two-story stucco and Spanish-tiled-roof house with a giant front lawn designed to blend in with the desert landscape.

"Damn. I never get tired of seeing this place." Isa scooted toward the car door as it opened.

I stepped out first and offered her my hand so she could exit. When she took it, I tugged her toward me, bringing her in for a kiss.

When I pulled back, the heat was back in her blue eyes. "Want me to build you something like this?"

She shook her head. "No, our penthouse is perfect. I'm a city girl. Plus, I prefer gifts of deadly weapons versus mansions."

She patted her handbag, where she'd placed the pistol I'd bought her from a dealer near the range.

"You're definitely the perfect woman for me."

That got a smile to touch her lips.

"Are the two of you going to stand outside all day

making moony eyes at each other or are you coming in? There's a pregnant woman in the house who's about to come out and drag you inside," Penny shouted from the open front door.

Isa

I couldn't help but smile at Penny's snarky tone.

"We were discussing weapons," I called back. "You know how I like weapons."

Penny snorted and raised her brows toward Sebastian. "I'm sure you like the weapon he's carrying."

The woman was incorrigible.

"Obviously. I wouldn't have married him otherwise."

Penny rolled her eyes. "And you're positive it had nothing to do with some archaic European tradition of arranged marriages?"

"Absolutely not."

"Come on, let me introduce you to my baby brother, Adrian. I'm sure you know he and Sebastian go way back. They studied together at UNLV."

Adrian came over, and I couldn't help but take in his sculpted male beauty. The man was built and was almost too good looking, especially with the added effect of the dark shadows of his beard and a slight scar on his chin.

Damn, Ana had done good.

"Hello, Isa. I didn't get a chance to meet you when you came last time. I heard you're a bit of a card shark. Hopefully I'll get to see your skills in action."

"You never know."

As I moved into the house, I paused and watched Adrian fist-bump with Sebastian and then hug him.

"It's good to see you again." Sebastian smacked Adrian's back.

"It's been too long."

Sebastian's tone changed to almost a whisper. "I'd gotten used to seeing your ugly mug almost every week."

"It's better this way. I'll do what I have to for Ana. She's still working through what happened."

Sebastian knew about what happened to Ana? We were seriously going to have to talk.

"Did you tell her?" Adrian asked as they stepped back from each other.

Sebastian shook his head and then I heard Adrian mutter, "Idiot. It's your grave."

What was that about?

Before I could question the men on the unusual exchange, I was engulfed in a plethora of hugs and welcomes. Hagen, Pierce, Zack, and Henna swarmed me.

It was like coming home being around them. They were happy to see me and welcomed me in. It had been like this from the first time I'd met them. The brothers especially were reputed to be hard men but with me they were nothing but affectionate. At first, I'd thought it was because

I was their half sister Ana's friend, but then I realized they genuinely liked me.

Now, anytime one of the Lykaioses made a trip close to Germany, we met up. Of all of them, Hagen was the one who came to visit the most often and had advised me as I'd started my clubs.

"Where's Ana?" I tried to look over the shoulders of the men but it was like trying to see over a wall of over-six-foot-tall men. "You guys are great to look at and all but I need to see my girl."

"I'm the soon-to-be beached whale over here," Ana said, and she came into view as her brothers shifted.

"You'll never be a beached whale. You're absolutely gorgeous." I walked over to her and wrapped my arms around her.

I wasn't lying. Ana looked as if she could have walked off the pages of a high-end maternity catalog. Her unique golden-hued skin that she'd inherited from her Indian father and Greek mother added to her beauty. She was a real-life fertility goddess.

I was literally in a house of people who looked like they were created by the Greek gods.

"You're good for my ego. I may not let you go home."

"Where Isa goes, I go." Sebastian came up behind me.

Then he did a silent conversation thing with Ana. Ana's amber, almost tiger-like eyes grew wide and then flashed with annoyance before she shook her head.

"What am I missing?" I asked both of them.

Almost as soon as the question was out, the pieces fell into place.

Sebastian had told me he'd worked with Bri. I'd assumed it was as an informant or consultant as I was. Which couldn't be true if he saw Adrian nearly every week until recently. Then there was the fact Sebastian knew about what went down on Ana's last assignment. The only reason I found out some of the details was because it was in the file for some of the artwork I'd had to evaluate after the case closed. Even then, my information was limited and I could only guess as to what might have happened to Ana.

Sebastian clearly knew more details than I did.

This meant one thing—Sebastian was the man who'd helped rescue Ana when her assignment went south and she was kidnapped. The assignment Ana had been on was a joint Solon/Interpol/CIA case. Ana was the Solon contact, and Adrian was the CIA component. Which left Sebastian.

He was Interpol.

My husband, a mob boss, was an agent for an intelligence agency. Now the favor he'd done for Bri made sense. He'd helped save one of her agents. Ana.

I studied Sebastian's worried face.

There was still something I was missing. I looked between Ana, Adrian, and Sebastian.

"I think the three of us need to go into another room and have a conversation." Ana glared at Sebastian as she tucked her arm in mine and pulled me toward the back of the house and an open door.

The four of us moved into a room that looked like a library.

Once we were inside and the door was locked, I blurted out, "You're Interpol."

"Yes," Sebastian answered.

"I know Ana is Solon." I glanced at her.

"Former. I left."

Then I moved my attention to Adrian. "And you're CIA."

"Retired."

I walked over to a window overlooking the desert. "And the three of you were on Ana's last case."

I tried to remember everything I'd heard and read in the case analysis. They'd been on an assignment to stop a sex-trafficking ring. Ana was supposed to pose as one of the victims when she'd been kidnapped. Two agents had gone in pretending to be buyers.

"You slept with Ana. Didn't you?"

A wave of jealousy hit me, making me want to throw up. Ana was someone I respected, who I looked up to. She was literally a badass spy.

"Yes." Sebastian took a step toward me but I shook my head.

He couldn't touch me right now.

"How many times?"

"Once."

I caught Ana rubbing her belly with worry etched all over her face and Adrian's hand on her shoulder.

She'd gotten pregnant during that time, there was no doubt in my mind.

"Is there any chance the baby is yours?"

Surprise flashed on Sebastian's features. "No. Without a doubt."

"Absolutely not," Adrian added but I ignored him, my focus on Sebastian.

"Why didn't you tell me?"

"I didn't know how to tell you I slept with one of your close friends as part of my work without revealing who I worked for or hurting you."

"I would have rather heard it from you than learned it like this." A tear slipped down my cheek. "Haven't you learned that keeping something from me is just as hurtful as lying?"

"Baby, there are always things I'm not going to be able to tell you."

I clenched my jaw. "I don't want to hear it. There's a fucking difference between having slept with my girlfriend and running the business."

He had to believe I was an idiot. I knew the rules, I knew when it came to the family some things I'd never know.

I looked at Ana again. "You stalled my investigation into Sebastian. You knew I was going to marry him."

She nodded. "I didn't have a choice. But I promise, I gave you everything that was available on him that wasn't classified."

"And telling me you fucked my soon-to-be husband

was classified." I couldn't hide the hurt or anger in my tone.

"Isa, you know the way it works." Ana sighed. "Some cases require us to do things we wouldn't think of doing in the real world. We were undercover. We had no choice in what happened. We had an audience and had to make it look real."

I cringed thinking of what she'd had to experience.

Logically I knew some agents went so deep they lived out what they'd been sent to do. Ana had been kidnapped and sold. Adrian and Sebastian had done whatever it took to get her back.

"I'm just so tired of the secrets."

"Isa, our lives are all about secrets." Sebastian came to stand in front of me. "Can we talk alone?"

I nodded. And in my peripheral vision, I saw Ana and Adrian get up.

Was I being too dramatic?

Maybe I was.

Maybe it was jealousy fueling the hurt.

No, I'd been lied to. Again.

It pissed me off that someone I knew had seen Sebastian naked, had felt his touch, knew what it was like to have him deep inside her. But it was more that Sebastian had kept it from me. Another check in the "I have no idea if the man I love is real or a figment of my imagination" column.

"Isa?"

I looked at Ana.

"If it makes you feel better, I'll let you sleep with

Adrian."

"The hell she will." Sebastian's roar was almost comical, and I would have laughed if I wasn't so pissed.

"Ana, babe," Adrian said with a slight amused tone. "I don't think that's a solution. Besides, if my dick goes anywhere near another woman, you'll cut it off."

"I suppose you're right. The thought does make me stabby."

They walked out of the library, still talking.

Sebastian went to lock the door and then came back to me.

"We need to get something straight." He towered over me. "There's only one woman I plan to fuck, as you put it, for the rest of my life. And that's you."

I opened my mouth to argue that point, but shut it. He was right. Being jealous of something that happened before we knew each other was ridiculous. I'd had relationships and lovers before him. Though I wasn't sure I'd ever want Sebastian to meet any of them.

"Nothing to say?"

"So, do we just pretend nothing ever happened with you and Ana?"

"It's the way it works. Once a case is over, we debrief and walk away." He cupped my jaw, tilting it up.

I stared into his dark irises. The pain of another lie made me question whether it was possible to have any sort of real relationship with him.

"Isa, when Jonas forced my hand to accept our marriage, I was angry and determined to live my life as I always had. Which meant all my focus was on my job and completing my assignments by any means necessary.

"I wasn't expecting to feel this way about you. But now that you're mine, my priorities have changed. I'm never letting you go. You're it for me."

This wasn't a declaration of love, but it was something.

I was so tired of being in the dark. I needed things to be transparent between us. It wasn't as if leaving him was an option.

"I need one promise from you."

"What?" A slight crease formed between his brows.

"No more lying to me."

"I haven't lied to you."

"Lies by omission are still lies."

He nodded. "Then I guess I'd better tell you one more thing."

"You mean why you so readily agreed to leave Germany? Or how you had a plane, destination, and itinerary ready in less than an hour without worrying about the operations of your organization?"

Sebastian winced. "Noticed that, did you?"

"I'm not stupid, and your actions would have been obvious to a blind man. What's going on, Baz?"

"The last thing I'd believe about you is that you're stupid. Let's sit down for this." He led me to a set of chairs near us.

Instead of letting me take my own seat, he sat, and then pulled me onto his lap. He set a hand across my thighs and the other on my back, pulling me against him.

He was quiet as if waiting for some sign.

"Spill it," I ordered.

He inhaled deep. "Jonas arranged for my mother's murder."

That wasn't what I expected to hear. "What? How did you find out?"

"We discovered it after I threw Jonas out of his house."

"Why didn't you tell me sooner? You seemed fine this whole time."

"I've spent the last ten years mourning my mother and sister. My gut told me Jonas was involved, but I tried to ignore it. Knowing the truth doesn't change the fact they're gone. In a sense it was closure."

His words seemed so calm, but there was no way he wasn't affected by the news that his father was responsible for his mother and sister's deaths.

Sometimes it surprised me how much Sebastian was like Papa. Papa hadn't shed a tear when *Opa* passed away. It was business as usual. The only indication Papa missed *Opa* was the way he'd touch *Opa*'s picture every morning as he passed it in the hallway.

"Closure doesn't mean you don't feel. The news had to have been devastating."

"I won't lie, my heart aches from the loss of them, but letting the pain overwhelm me won't bring them back. It's the threat to you that has me wanting to kill Jonas with my bare hands."

"Threat?"

"Jonas followed us from the beginning. He had pictures

of us at Emma's and at my club. He knew we were together before our wedding. And with you, he found the perfect leverage against me. You're the one person I'd tear the world down to protect."

From the intensity of his words and the way he held my gaze, I knew he was telling the truth.

Breaking eye contact, I said, "And?"

"And he negotiated to sell you to Malkovich, the head of a Russian organization trying to gain a larger territory in Germany, in exchange for a favor of support when Jonas tried to take back the family from me." He clenched his jaw. "As of right now, there are orders to take you by any means necessary and deliver you to Malkovich's family home outside Moscow."

"I don't understand. Why would he want me? As far as I know, I haven't had any dealings with any Russian in my work."

"According to the transcripts we found of conversations Jonas recorded, Malkovich wants you to breed the next generation of his line. You come from one of the most powerful families in Europe. He's trying to establish a stronghold in Germany, and you seemed to be his key."

What the fuck?

"Not happening. There is no way in hell I would ever let him touch me."

Sebastian's arms tightened around me. "If the bastard got his hands on you, he'd use any means necessary to make sure it happened."

A chill went down my spine. Whoever this bastard was would resort to raping me to achieve whatever demented vision he had.

"And so, when I insisted we leave the country, you agreed, seeing it as a win-win without telling me the whole of it."

"I didn't want to scare you."

"I was already scared. I did have a crazy conversation with Bri where she told me there was a hit out on you."

He shook his head. "I wish she'd kept that shit to herself. There's been some hit or another out on me since I was in grade school. It's part of the life we lead."

"I have a question. How does being a Weber play into your work for Interpol?"

"My connections get them into places where they'd never have access, and they leave me the hell alone to run my business. It's a mutually beneficial arrangement."

"But you're an agent and the..." I wasn't sure how to put it.

"...head of an organized syndicate." He finished my sentence. "There are lines most of the organizations in Europe won't cross. I just happen to go after the ones who do."

He was talking about sex trafficking. That was the one piece of information Ana had provided me. Sebastian Weber had a no-tolerance view of anyone involved in that world. So it made sense for him to have been involved in Ana's assignment.

It still didn't sit well with me that my husband had slept

with one of my friends, but I'd have to get over it. From the way Adrian acted toward Sebastian, he had no issues with the past. All indications showed they were still friends, even if they couldn't run in the same circles anymore.

"Have you left anything out? Anything that will make me all stabby, as Ana put it?"

"No."

I wanted to believe there couldn't be any more, but then again, his job was to keep secrets.

"I mean it. There's only so much I can take."

He leaned in. "You asked for a promise. Here it is. I promise never to lie to you with omission or otherwise. If I can't tell you something, I'll say it point blank."

I wasn't sure how I felt about the latter part, but it was the best I was going to get. At least now I knew what he meant by wearing many faces. Organized crime boss, Interpol agent, and Baz. As long as my Baz was there under it all, I'd handle it.

The trust would have to come in time.

"Okay."

He smiled, and it reached his eyes for the first time since we entered the library.

My heart skipped a beat.

I grabbed his face in my hands and pulled him toward me for a kiss.

This marriage thing was way more complicated than I could ever have imagined.

CHAPTER EIGHTEEN

Isa

We arrived back at Ida a little before eight in the evening. What had originally been planned as a brunch turned into a surprisingly relaxing and fun day of food, poker, and laughter.

It was enlightening to see Sebastian interact with everyone. He shared a history with the Lykaios-Kipos family that went back over a decade. Plus seeing the easy way Adrian and Sebastian interacted eased any lingering jealousy I'd had about the whole Ana and Sebastian thing.

What surprised me most was that no one seemed fazed by how abruptly we'd gone into the library and then returned an hour later. It was as if it was a regular occurrence in the house. Then again, this was a very animated and intense family.

Hopefully we'd get to enjoy another of these gatherings before Sebastian and I had to get back home.

Just as the driver pulled into the residence driveway, Sebastian asked, "Are you tired?"

I cocked my head to the side. "No. What do you have planned?"

I knew it wasn't sex. For some reason, the man wanted to keep me in a state of lady blue balls.

"I want to revisit something we started during our wedding night but never finished."

My heartbeat was a drum in my chest and head. Maybe this was going to lead to some hot monkey sex, after all.

"Are you willing?"

Anxiety and excitement coursed in my blood as did the anticipation of what he planned.

"Yes."

"Then follow me." He offered me his hand and we exited the car as soon as the door opened. We walked past the front desk and into the main area of the opulent hotel.

"Where are we going?"

He continued to guide me past slot machines and card tables. "Do you trust me?"

"Yes," I answered and then added, "With my body."

It wasn't the answer he wanted, but we still had things to work through. Too much had happened for me to blindly trust him. Our conversation from earlier in the day had shifted something between us. I knew he wouldn't go back on his word. He would keep me informed.

I wasn't naive enough to believe I'd know everything

that went on in his world. I knew from growing up with Papa, sometimes it was better not to know.

Complete trust would come in time. All I cared about was that my Baz would always be there underneath.

Sebastian stopped, turning toward me. The intensity of his gaze had my breath catching. He wasn't upset with what I'd said. He accepted it.

"One day, you'll trust me with everything." He cupped my face. "Just know you're mine, Isa. To possess, to protect, to cherish. Your pleasure is the balm to my black soul."

I gripped one of his wrists as the other settled on his chest. "Your soul isn't as dark as you believe it is."

His easy acknowledgement of my feelings cracked the wall I'd started to build around my heart since I discovered the truth of what happened on the mission with Ana.

"So, you aren't still mad at me for denying you an orgasm?"

I couldn't help but smile. "Are you mad at me for leaving you with a raging hard-on?"

"Not as long as I get to end tonight inside you. Which I plan to, and we're both going to come harder than ever before."

"Well when you put it that way, I have no objections of any kind for what's ahead."

His mouth curved at the corners, making his gorgeous looks even more staggering.

The elevator doors opened as we reached the main floor of the hotel.

He stepped back, taking my hand in his and thumbing

the diamond of my wedding ring. "Then follow me, Mrs. Kohl."

"After you, Mr. Kohl."

The second we stepped out into the casino area I was awestruck. Rows and rows of slot machines lined one area; another was filled with tables with all variety of games from poker and blackjack to roulette.

It was bright, with clean lines, and modern. The only contrasts of color were splashes of rich amber. Then I remembered the hotel had been designed as homage to Penny before Hagen and Penny were even an item. The man built a hundred-million-dollar project around the woman of his dreams.

"It's pretty incredible," Sebastian said. "You should see the one Henna built. It puts this one to shame."

"We should make a plan to check it out tomorrow. The last time I was here, Henna promised me a day at her over-the-top spa once the resort was operational."

A spa day sounded so incredible after the roller coaster of emotions I'd suffered over the last week. Hell, what I'd gone through today.

He stared at me.

"What?"

"I like seeing you like this."

"Like what?"

"Relaxed, not so in control."

"I'm pretending to be someone else. I can let my hair down."

"I want you to be this way with me all the time."

"You know it isn't possible. The second we step foot on German soil, things change."

"They don't have to."

I pulled him to a stop and set a hand on his chest. "I really get it now. We have to play our roles. But I'll make you a promise."

He set his palm over mine. "What's that?"

"When we're alone, when eyes aren't on us, we'll be Isa and Baz. Two people who fell hard and fast and are perfect for each other."

Something flashed in his dark brown gaze. "Deal. Now I want to show you something I know you'll enjoy and most people don't even know exists at this hotel."

We took a path filled with the scents of fresh flowers and plants that I assumed led to the botanical garden Penny had told me about on my last visit.

We approached a well-dressed giant of a man standing by an ornate wall.

He studied us for a second before asking, "Name?"

"Sebastian Kohl."

The man checked his phone, then nodded and pressed his palm to a plate on the wall. A section shifted, revealing a dimly lit hallway.

Well, I wasn't expecting that to happen. But then again, this was a Lykaios property and they were known for their unique designs.

"Enjoy your evening."

The distant sound of music echoing told me there was some sort of lounge on the other side. The decor and the discreet location of the place distinctly reminded me of Sebastian's club.

That's when it hit me. Sebastian was taking me to a kink club.

The hallway opened up into a room filled with couples and groups enjoying cocktails and food, but what surprised me was the way they were dressed. Women were clad in everything from gowns to barely there lingerie.

"They allow alcohol in the clubs here?"

I remembered Lilly telling me there was no alcohol on the premises at Sebastian's club. The only drinks available were soda and mocktails.

"Only in the lounge. Anyone taking part in any scene has to take a breathalyzer. They want everyone to be sober when they play. It's for everyone's safety."

"Are we going to have a drink?"

"No."

My heartbeat accelerated. "Does that mean we're going to play?"

Sebastian set his hand on my lower back, almost like a brand through the material of my dress, and leaned into my ear and whispered, "Yes, it does. I'm going to make that fantasy you have in your head a reality. And then when I'm done..." He trailed off.

"What will you do when you're done?"

"I'm going to fuck you stupid."

"Oh." A low ache pulsed in my core. "I can deal with that."

"I'm glad you can."

Sebastian continued up a set of stairs and what I saw when we reached the top had my blood heating.

Scenes of all types were in play all around us, in various rooms opened to viewing from clear glass windows. There were couples in the midst of wax play while others engaged in full-on sex.

This club was very much like Sebastian's but on a larger scale.

The one that drew my attention was a man tied to a table while his Mistress caressed him with black gloves.

I knew what they were—Vampire gloves. Lilly had told me about them. They had these tiny needles, more like thumbtacks in the leather. They were meant to stimulate the skin, to heighten arousal but not hurt. Well, unless the user wanted them to.

The man arched into his Mistress's touch and his erection pushed up the fabric of his pants.

"Do you want me to get a pair?" Sebastian slid an arm around my waist pulling me back, much the same way he'd done the first night we'd been together.

"Yes."

"I'll have to remember that. Are you ready for your own scene?"

A thought flashed in my mind. "It's not public, is it?"

He cupped my neck and tilted my face up so he could look into my eyes. "No one gets to see you come but me."

The possessiveness of his words had goosebumps prickling down my spine.

"Now, follow me." He released his hold on my throat and guided me toward a back corner.

He typed in a code on the keypad and a hidden door opened. We took another hallway and then entered a room lit by candles.

My breath immediately grew unsteady, and the arousal I felt pulsing earlier now grew to a full-on throb in my clit.

Sebastian closed the door but didn't lock it. I wasn't sure there even was a lock. I knew the rules from the information Lilly had given me. Doors were never locked, just in case things got out of hand and safe words weren't respected.

That made me ask, "Are there people going to be listening to us?"

"It's part of their job, baby. They have no idea who's in the room. All they do is make sure the people in the room are safe and everything is consensual."

"Isn't that the same thing as being in public?"

"No, baby. To the people listening, it isn't voyeurism as it is in the public scenes. To them we're like any other members of the club—nameless, faceless patrons. The only time we'd ever come in contact with them is if they felt like the scene needed to end."

"But we speak German. How will they know what we're saying?"

Sebastian snaked an arm around me and pulled me forward. "The Lykaioses have enough technology in this place to know when, where, and what is said. Language isn't a barrier. Adrian is a genius like his sister and the mastermind behind every piece of technology under the Lykaios umbrella."

Before I could ask another question, Sebastian covered my lips with a finger. "No more talking unless I ask you a question."

The change in his voice had all the hairs on the back of my neck prickling.

"When I release you, you will strip and kneel on the pillow by the cross."

I glanced in the direction of the St. Andrew's cross.

This was really going to happen. I'd wanted it. Wanted to feel the euphoria of letting someone else completely control my pleasure. Sebastian had dominated me from the beginning but there was always a push and pull between us. Here, I'd hand over the reins.

"Do you understand, Isa?" Sebastian's question pulled me from my thoughts.

I swallowed and nodded.

"Give me the words."

"Yes, I understand."

"What's your safe word?"

Deception came to mind, but then I pushed it away. It no longer fit. Then I knew the word. It made sense. Others had forced us together, but the connection we had from the beginning was instantaneous.

I looked up at him. "Destiny."

He fisted my hair, pulling me in for a deep, mind-numbing kiss before releasing me and moving to the back of the room.

"Strip and kneel by the cross."

It was as if the energy of the room completely shifted into something I couldn't describe but had every nerve in my body on high alert.

I reached behind me to lower the zipper of my dress, stepping out of it and setting it on a nearby table. Then I removed my bra and underwear.

When I reached down to undo the buckles of my sandals, Sebastian said, "Leave them."

My nipples pebbled in response to the rough timbre of his voice, and my skin prickled with goosebumps.

I moved toward the pillow and lowered onto my knees. I wasn't sure how to sit, so I positioned my thighs slightly apart and bottom on my heels as I'd seen some of the women do in the public scenes.

"Beautiful."

His praise felt like a balm to my unsteady nerves.

I lowered my gaze, staring at the floor.

"Look at me. I don't want you to ever feel like you can't look me in the eyes. We're equals, Isa. This is you giving me your control in exchange for the pleasure I can give you. Remember, this is all about you. You're the one with the power."

He moved toward me. "The next time you kneel before me like this, we're going to finish what you started in the jet's cabin."

I almost smiled but kept my face calm.

Sebastian offered me his hand, and I slid my palm over his. He walked me over to the St. Andrew's cross, positioning my back against the cushioned center. He lifted both of my arms, strapping them together with the cuffs hanging from the top, and then bent to fasten my ankles to the lower beams.

Now I understood why he wanted me to wear my heels. It gave me the height I needed to be comfortable without stretching my body too much.

"At any time you feel it's too much, you say your safe word. We'll stop, no questions."

He'd stopped when I'd used my safe word on our wedding night, so I trusted him. He wouldn't push me any further than I could handle. When it came to sex and my life, I could trust him completely. It was everything else we had to work on.

"I know you will."

His features softened and he ran a thumb over my lower lip before giving me a soft kiss. "I'm not good with words, Isa. Just know I've never given this much of myself to anyone."

My throat burned, hearing the emotion in his words. One day I could only hope he gave me all of him.

"I do know."

"I'll protect you with my dying breath."

"I'll protect you too."

"It'll never come to that." He kissed me again and the

tenderness from a second before disappeared, replaced by a mask of complete control.

He reached over to a table near the cross, picking up a flogger, much like the one the Dom had used on his submissive at the club. The handle was black and the multitude of leather tails were in shades of red.

"Are you ready?"

"Yes."

"Then we begin."

I expected the sting of the flogger. Instead I felt the smooth handle rub over my nipples, circling each and then moving lower until it slid between the lips of my sex, grazing my clit.

My pussy flooded with desire, and a moan escaped my lips.

He teased my body with the handle for…I wasn't sure how long, lulling me into a half-focused state.

When the first strike came, I wasn't expecting it and gasped, jerking my bound arms and crying out as the pain shocked my system. Just as fast, it morphed into a dull ache.

"Breathe, baby."

I released the breath I hadn't realized I was holding.

My body was on fire and I wanted more.

"More, Baz."

The next smack of the flogger had my mind clouding with pain and pleasure at the same time. Had I ever felt anything so incredible? The sting was something I'd crave again and again.

Sebastian began a tempo of strikes that had me arching into each kiss of the leather straps. Every inch of my exposed skin was on fire and burned with pleasure-pain unlike anything I could have imagined.

"Do you want me to stop? Just say the word."

Was he crazy?

My pussy dripped with my need for this man and what he was doing to me with the flogger.

"No. Please I need more." I pled with both my words and eyes.

That was when I noticed the bulge pressing against Sebastian's pants. He was as affected by this as I was.

"As you wish, love."

He continued to make me mindless with the kiss of the flogger. It was as if I would orgasm any moment.

"Please Baz. I want...I want." I thrashed against the cross, lost in mindless need.

Sebastian dropped the flogger, and the press of the front of his body to my aching skin was so intense, tears streamed down my face. "What do you want?"

"You, please. Inside me."

"As you wish," he repeated, stepping back to shuck his clothes and returning when he was naked.

He pressed the thick hard head of his cock to my sopping pussy.

"Fuck. You're dripping." He pushed in all the way before pulling out and thrusting back in.

He fucked me hard and fast, catapulting me into release.

My core clamped down on his pistoning cock, quivering and spasming.

His pace was unrelenting and kept me rolling from one orgasm to another.

By the time Sebastian came I was mindless and lost in the most incredible experience of my life.

CHAPTER NINETEEN

Sebastian

I held Isa close as we exited the club. She was still riding the high of our scene. I'd allowed her to nap in my arms for an hour after I'd lowered her from the cross and tended to her body, bathing and dressing her. We'd had a light meal to help her with the crash she'd experience from the rush of endorphins coursing through her body.

This woman accepted me, all parts of me, even the parts that went completely against the world we lived in. Whatever the reason *Opa* and Mama arranged my marriage to Isa, I was eternally grateful.

She really was the perfect woman for me.

While Isa slept, I tapped my Interpol contacts to see if they could help with the threat on Isa and keep an eye on Jonas.

The only way he would ever gain back power was to take me out, and to accomplish that task he'd need a man on the inside of my organization, and I'd cleaned house. Only the most trusted had information on my whereabouts.

If there were rats in the infrastructure, they weren't in the higher ranks and would have limited information. I'd eventually weed them out.

For now, I'd give Isa time with her friends, who happened to be my friends. Then, I'd set the plan into motion to take down Jonas, the Russians, or anyone who threatened us.

"Baz," Isa said as we exited the hotel and went to the side walkway leading to the fountain show about to start at another resort on the strip.

"Yes?"

"I want our marriage to work. I don't want the type of marriage your parents had."

The thought of the pain and suffering my mother had endured made me want to find Jonas and shoot him in the head.

"That is one promise I can readily make you. Outside of being arranged, we have nothing in common with what Mama and Jonas had. There was never a day of love between them. He never felt an ounce for my mother what I feel for you."

"What do you feel for me?"

There it was. She wanted the words.

I stared into the blue pools of her eyes. "I love you, Isa. More than you could ever know."

"I know you do." A smile broke across her face. "I just wanted you to say the words."

"You made me go through that, and you knew what you meant to me?"

She leaned up on tiptoes and kissed me. "Don't look so put out. A woman needs to hear these things."

She adjusted her clutch and tucked her arms around my waist, burying her face against my chest.

I waited to hear her words again, but they never came. I couldn't help but feel a sense of disappointment.

She loved me. I knew she did but I'd hurt her by keeping things from her, and it was going to take some time to earn her trust back and get her to admit she loved me again.

"Come on, baby. We still have a five-minute walk before we get to the spot with the best view."

Isa stepped out of my hold and tucked her arm into mine.

We hadn't taken two steps when Isa's eyes grew big and she said, "What's Kane doing here?"

I shifted my gaze to where she looked and took in the man who managed a few of my businesses. He was supposed to be in the middle of a quarterly review of expenses, not a vacation. And it was too coincidental for him to be in Las Vegas at the same time Isa and I were here.

The only way he would know our location was if Lilly had told him. Lilly wouldn't betray Isa.

"He has a gun!" I heard our bodyguards shout. "Move!"

Before I could react, Isa reached into her purse, pulled out the pistol we'd bought earlier in the day, took aim, and shot.

At the same moment, we were both tackled to the ground as more gunfire erupted around us.

"Boss, stay down."

Shouts echoed all around us until it went silent. It seemed as if the never-ending noise of Vegas quieted.

"We have him," came an American voice. "The area is secure."

He had to be one of the Lykaios brothers' men.

The body on my back lifted and I shifted to move off Isa. "Baby. Are you all right?"

"I'm okay. I'm okay," she wheezed out. "Baz, I called Lilly today to check on a project."

She was thinking the same thing I was. Lilly, or someone, had tipped Kane off.

"I know Lilly didn't do this. She's naive. She…" Isa trailed off as her eyes closed.

That was when I saw blood on my hand where it rested on her side.

Kane shot her. The motherfucker had shot her.

Everything inside me died.

———

There was one thing I was sure of, Kane Mancheski was a dead man. As were the people he worked for. If Isa wasn't lying here, motionless, I'd be in the room getting every bit of information out of the fucker. I'd trusted the bastard for years. Hell, his father had been a trusted member of *Opa*'s inner circle.

Instead of showing loyalty to the family, he'd betrayed us. And worst of all, he'd used Isa as a way to get to me.

I clutched Isa's hand as she lay in the makeshift clinic Ana and Adrian had created for us in one wing of their Vegas desert mansion.

They, along with the Lykaios brothers, had given us the cover we needed to escape the chaos that ensued on the strip following the shooting. Police had swarmed the area as had the media. But thankfully Adrian had used his tech skills to wipe all video surveillance for the vicinity and had gone as far as to wash any evidence of Isa's blood from the concrete where we'd fallen.

"She's going to be okay, Weber," Adrian said as he entered the room. "The bullet went through clean. This is normal after major blood loss. Plus, she has a head injury from the impact of the fall."

I glared at him. "Did it make any difference to you when Ana was hurt? Tell me you didn't want to resurrect the fucker even though Ana had already killed him so you could do it yourself."

I couldn't hide the rage coursing through my blood.

"I won't say that. I'd end the bastard again for touching her. You have to understand Isa is strong, just like Ana."

"Did you get anything out of the asshole?" I clenched the fist of my other hand.

After my soldiers had hustled Isa and me from the very visible walkway around Ida, my time was lost in making sure Isa would live. I knew Adrian would use any means necessary to get the information out of Mancheski.

"You're not going to like this."

"As if anything about this whole situation is something I'm going to like."

"Jonas and Malkovich are behind this."

"That's not news to me."

"No, this was a setup from the beginning. Mancheski's mother is Malkovich's distant cousin. He targeted Isa's friend Lilly before Jonas forced the marriage on you."

"Why would the fucker do that?"

"I'm going to tell you the story Mancheski told us and you tell me if it makes sense."

Fine. I stared at Isa, who hadn't budged an inch since I'd laid her on the bed yesterday.

Over the next twenty minutes, Adrian relayed a history of my family I knew but not in detail.

I was well aware my mother and Jonas's marriage was forced upon them but I hadn't realized Mama had done it out of desperation. Her wedding to Andrew was supposed to be the week he was killed, and then shortly afterward, she found out she was pregnant.

With me.

According to the story Adrian told, Jonas had assumed I was his child until my sister Hannah was born. She looked exactly like him, whereas I looked like the spitting image of my uncle Andrew.

This bit of information should have felt like a blow to everything I knew, but seemed to only give weight to the reason I knew a man who was supposed to be my father hated me.

Jonas had treated me like some unwanted burden. The only time he ever handled me as more than garbage had been when *Opa* was around. *Opa*, on the other hand, had treated me like his heir from my earliest childhood memory, even going as far as putting my training in the business before that of Jonas's.

"What does any of this have to do with the hit on Isa? I know Jonas had plans to hand her over to Malkovich."

Adrian shook his head. "The hit wasn't on Isa. It was on you. In fact, as of an hour ago, we found at least ten contracts out in the market."

"Then what does Isa have to do with this?"

"Isa was the reward for carrying out the hit. Malkovich wanted Isa from the time her family made her debut into society. She was just as stunning at sixteen as she is now. Apparently, Benz took offense to Malkovich wanting to negotiate a marriage for his teenage daughter, especially with the reputation Malkovich had for his treatment of his mistresses. Benz may be a ruthless bastard, but he would never sell his only child to a fucker like Malkovich, no matter the reward. Isa is the reason for the Benz-Malkovich rivalry."

The thought of Malkovich even touching a hair on Isa's head was unfathomable.

"What does that have to do with our current situation? This makes no sense."

"Man, you can't be this dense. I get you're fucked up with Isa getting shot, but come on. You are the best strategist I know."

"Don't make me punch you, asshole. Just spit it out."

"Jonas gets shit as your uncle. You've been the Weber heir since your birth. Your grandfather knew it and your mother knew it. The marriage contract between you and Isa was to protect Isa from Malkovich and you from Jonas. Don't for one minute believe Jonas wasn't aware of the marriage contract until recently. This whole thing was too cleverly orchestrated."

I tried to process everything Adrian had said. Under the marriage contract, Jonas inherited millions. Without it, he got nothing outside of the trust fund *Opa* had created for each of his sons. He would remain the spare son. And Jonas wasn't the type of man to make way for himself without trading on the family name as Uncle Fredrik had done.

As my father, even if it was on paper, he would get what was due to him as a retired family head. By putting a hit out on me, he would get the money free and clear and return to the helm of the family structure.

Jonas wasn't the type to do the dirty work himself. He knew any link to him and my death would cause him more harm than good and open him up to retaliation from inside the Weber organization.

Money was the motivation for everything in Jonas's life. There was no doubt in my mind the hit on Mama was the result of him knowing I wasn't his child. He wanted to remove anyone who could prove the truth.

The bastard needed to die.

"My wife and Lilly were pawns in Jonas's game." I kept my voice calm, hoping it would stay the anger boiling inside me.

It was time to be rid of Jonas Weber for good. And Malkovich. That bastard was going to suffer the fall of his organization before I took care of him.

"Yes." Adrian ran a hand through his hair. "Fuck, I know what you're thinking."

"Don't even think about interfering."

First, I was going to take care of Mancheski and then I'd deal with Jonas and Malkovich. There were enough people sprinkled throughout the world who owed me a favor or two. I planned to collect.

"Dammit, Sebastian. You're Interpol, a fucking cop."

"Who's broken laws of nearly every country to make sure the assignment was completed."

Adrian released a resigned breath. "You know Ana's going to kick my ass."

"I'm not asking you to help. Stay with your pregnant wife. She needs you here."

"You got it wrong. She's going to kick my ass because she can't be part of it."

I smiled and knew Isa would probably have the same reaction. Thinking of her, I looked in her direction.

She still slept, the dark shadows under her eyes less visible. She needed her rest, and there was no way she could handle the journey home. The safest place for her was here, under the protection of a retired Solon agent. Pregnant or not, Ana was dangerous.

Then there were her brothers—they would never let anything happen to Isa.

"You know we're going to have to do a lot of groveling when we return to our wives," Adrian said, figuring out what I had planned and deciding to join in.

"Groveling leads to phenomenal sex. I'll take my chances."

CHAPTER TWENTY

Isa

"Come home, *Schatz*," Mama pled over the phone as I tied the belt of my coat and leaned against the balcony of my room in Ana's house.

After everything that had happened, I now had a better understanding of the reasons she and *Opa* had arranged my marriage to Sebastian. It was her way of protecting me. Her baby. Her only child.

I'd spent so much of the last eight months angry at her, and with one conversation with Sebastian, everything had disappeared. Our mothers and grandfathers had been trying to keep Sebastian and me alive.

It would have been great if I was aware of all that was going on at the time. It would have also been better to learn this information from my husband before he left on his "mission" as he'd put it.

But I couldn't fault him for that bit. I wasn't conscious at the time Adrian and Sebastian left to handle Jonas and Malkovich.

I hadn't woken until two days after Sebastian returned to Germany and then it had taken me another two weeks to recover from the gunshot wound and concussion.

Now it had been two full months since I'd seen Sebastian and Ana had seen Adrian. The constant worry for our men was exhausting. It was worse for Ana—she was almost due and experiencing some of the milestones of pregnancy without Adrian. She had her crazy family around her, but it wasn't the same as being with one's own husband.

"Soon, Mama."

"At least tell me where you are. Do you know how worried we are? *Oma* spends all her time at the chapel praying, and your father…" She paused as if trying to compose herself. "He isn't himself."

Sebastian had told me during one of my first conversations with him after he'd arrived in Germany that Papa had been ready to wage war on Malkovich when he learned I'd been shot. He'd gone as far as calling a meeting of all the heads of the allied families to garner support for a takeover without retaliation.

Thankfully Sebastian had talked Papa down from what could have been a very public and a very brutal fight with God knew how many casualties. Which meant the authorities would get involved and that would cause problems for everyone all around. Sebastian had convinced Papa to keep up the business-as-usual image, while Sebastian used their connections to topple Malkovich's organization from the inside out.

That was the extent of the information he'd given me. He wanted to keep me out of the loop.

I'd essentially gone into hiding. Confined to Ana and Adrian's property, with its state-of-the-art security and personnel. Truthfully, it wasn't a hardship to be at the mansion.

At least I was able to communicate with the staff of my clubs to discuss operations. I guess it helped that Sebastian made periodic visits to each venue to make sure everything was running smoothly.

I missed Sebastian, so much. And the sporadic calls weren't enough. I worried for him and what he was doing to make it safe for me again. He wouldn't stop until he reached his goal.

The time apart also made me realize I did trust him. With my life, my body, and my heart.

Since the last time we were together and he'd told me he loved me, he'd ended every call with those words.

I'd held back.

There was no doubt I loved him, but it scared me to say it and be hurt again.

"I'm sorry, Mama. I can't."

"Have you spoken to him?"

"Yes. He calls me nearly every night."

Though this time, he'd gone longer. Three days, in fact.

"So, the rumors are true. He's doing all of this for you."

"Doing all of what?"

From the information I researched daily, territory wars were in full swing throughout the major cities in Germany. They weren't wars as most people believed but strategically planned assaults on major players where the lowest number of casualties occurred. There was never any mess for the public to clean up, just an underlying knowledge that something happened.

"He hasn't told you?"

"Told me what?"

"Your father-in-law's body was found last night."

My stomach dropped. No matter if Jonas wasn't Sebastian's father or that he'd been responsible for the death of Sebastian's mother and sister, I wouldn't want his death on Sebastian's hands.

"How?"

"Malkovich. From what I heard, Malkovich blames Jonas for bringing war to his territory. Jonas's body washed up on the shore of the Spree River."

I shouldn't feel it was justice that his fate was the same as the one he let happen to his wife and daughter.

"What about Malkovich? Is he alive?"

"Yes, unfortunately, he's alive." The way Mama said that made me realize how much she hated the man.

"So, he gets away with what he did to us. For sending Kane after us. For what Kane did to Lilly?"

My heart ached for my best friend. She'd all but turned

into a recluse. She blamed herself for bringing Kane into our lives. A sweep of Lilly's apartment revealed multiple recording and transmitting devices. Without realizing it, Lilly had relayed key things about me and my relationship with Sebastian. It was something I wasn't sure Lilly would ever forgive herself for doing.

"No, he hasn't gotten away with it," a deep voice said behind me. "I made sure Malkovich won't be a problem now or in the future. And Kane, as you know, was handled by Lilly's father."

I froze and my skin prickled. "Mama, I have to go."

"What's going on? Are you safe?"

"Yes, I'm as safe as I can be." Without saying anything else, I hung up and turned.

Sebastian leaned against the doorframe of the balcony doors. There was a healing bruise on his temple and cheek. He'd grown out the light dusting of stubble he always carried to a full-blown beard, almost giving him a piratical edge.

"Baz." My voice cracked.

"You shot a man."

"Yes. I'd do it again."

His lips quirked at the edge. "As long as it's not me, I have no objection."

I took a step toward him, when he lifted a hand to stay me.

"I have one request."

"Okay."

"The next time I tell you I love you, you aren't allowed

to get shot. My heart can't take it. And…"

"And what?"

"You have to tell me you love me back."

"I have no problem with that." My lips trembled as the emotions of the last few weeks seemed to rush forth.

I never wanted to be apart from him again. Not like this, anyway.

Sebastian stalked toward me, engulfing me in his arms. "God, baby. I missed you."

My tears flowed free as I held on to Sebastian.

"I love you, Isa."

I wouldn't hold this from him again. He needed the words as much as I did.

I pulled back to look into his dark eyes. "I love you. More than you could ever know. The good, the bad, and the Baz."

A smile touched his lips. "And the Baz?"

He carried me to a chair overlooking the desert and sat down with me in his lap.

I couldn't help but return his smile. "Too much?"

"Not in the least." He cradled me against him, pressing my face into his chest.

"Did Adrian come back with you?"

"Yes. He's with Ana." He paused, smirked, and then said, "Groveling."

Ana had told me over the last few weeks that she was going to make Adrian work his way back into her good graces. Which meant sex in her book. Hopefully it wouldn't induce labor.

I pushed that thought back and focused on the man holding me to him.

"Speaking of groveling. I believe you need to do some."

"I just spent the last month cleaning up a territory war. I promise I haven't engaged in any activity that requires me to grovel."

"You did leave me without a word." I shifted my body so I could straddle him, settling one knee on each side of his thighs and my arms around his neck.

Sebastian gripped my waist. "I'd argue that you were asleep and weren't available for consultation."

"Those technicalities aren't important."

"How would you like me to grovel? You name it, I'll do it."

I thought about it for a second and then said, "I'd like another night at the club in Ida."

Heat entered Sebastian's eyes, sending a tingle deep in my core.

"How about the one you visited in Berlin? I know the owner."

I licked my lips and leaned forward to graze my mouth against his. "Let's play here today and then visit the one in Berlin tomorrow."

"Anything you want, *Prinzessin.* Your wish is my command."

THE END

GODS OF VEGAS BOOK 1

Read the first book in the Gods of Vegas Series:

www.books2read.com/masterofsin

It was always him...

The one I shouldn't want, shouldn't crave, the one who could destroy my carefully built life.

Hagen Lykaios was the essence of sin, indulgence, and danger - everything I knew to avoid.

All it took was one unexpected touch, and he consumed me, left me begging, needy, and hungry for more.

He said if I entered his world he would corrupt me, own me, and change all that I had ever known...and you know what? ***I went anyway.***

ABOUT SIENNA SNOW

Inspired by her years working in corporate America, Sienna loves to serve up stories woven around confident and successful women who know what they want and how to get it, both in – and out – of the bedroom.

Her heroines are fresh, well-educated, and often find love and romance through atypical circumstances. Sienna treats her readers to enticing slices of hot romance infused with empowerment and indulgent satisfaction.

Sienna loves the life of travel and adventure. She plans to visit even the farthest corners of the world and delight in experiencing the variety of cultures along the way. When she isn't writing or traveling, Sienna is working on her "happily ever after" with her husband and children.

Find out more about Sienna at www.siennasnow.com